GUNHAWK BLOOD

A Novel of the McCabes

Brad Dennison

Author of
TENNESSEE and *JOE McCABE*

Published by PINE BOOKSHELF
Buford, Georgia

Cover Design: Donna Dennison

Cover Art: Chris Steele

Editors: Martha Gulick
         Megan Dennison

Copy Editors: Loretta Yike
              Doug Yike

Many thanks to artist Chris Steele for generously granting us permission for the use of his painting *High Meadow* for the cover art to this book. His work can be viewed on his website: https://pixels.com/featured/high-meadow-chris-steele.html

The excerpt from the Novel *Little Women* by Louisa May Alcott is in public domain.

This one goes out to my uncle, Robert Dennison. He was one of my strongest influences when I was growing up. He passed from this Earth fifteen years ago at the age of 89, but I miss him still.

GUNHAWK BLOOD

PART ONE

1

HIRAM McCABE ARRIVED in town without any fanfare. He wasn't expecting any, but it did seem strange to step off the train in a town where much of his family lived and find no one waiting to greet him. No hugs. No handshakes. Only strangers greeting other strangers.

Hiram had a carpet bag in one hand. He carried no other luggage. He figured he would simply buy anything else he needed. After all, he didn't know how long he would be here. His business partner asked him to come here and said he would meet him within a few days. That was all he said. So here Hiram was.

He was in a string tie, and his gray jacket and pinstriped trousers were made of silk. On his head was perched a matching gray bowler.

He was not a self-styled cowboy, as were his father and brothers, forever wearing riding boots. His father wore boots to the table for breakfast. Hiram was in shoes, the leather of which shined. He didn't have a gunbelt buckled about his hips, like his father and brothers also would have done. He carried a small Smith and Wesson .22 seven-shot revolver in a holster built into his jacket.

His father had taught him how to shoot. After all, his father was the brother of Johnny McCabe, the nearly legendary gunfighter. Books were being written about Johnny. There had been a stage play in Chicago. When people heard the name *McCabe*, Hiram found they grew starry-eyed and wanted to know if he was related to *the* Johnny McCabe, or to Dusty or Tom McCabe. Tom was Hiram's brother and Dusty their cousin, and both were gaining a reputation on their own. Tom was the marshal of the frontier town where Hiram now found himself.

A porter on the train asked him if he was related to *the* McCabes. Hiram thought of saying, "Yes, I'm the one they all hate. The evil one." But instead he just shook his head.

When Christmas rolled around each year, did Hiram receive Christmas cards from his father or Tom or their younger brother Danny? No. Not that Hiram sent any, but that was beside the point. When his legendary uncle was in California the previous summer, did he visit Hiram? The answer was equally no. Hiram heard his uncle was in town only days after the man had left.

Not that Hiram necessarily wanted to see him, but every so often, when Hiram had a moment of weakness, when he was sitting alone by the fire with a glass of scotch in hand, the fact that he was alone, with no family who cared if he even existed, weighed a little heavy on him.

Of course, there had been Mother. Hiram had been her favorite. But the woman essentially died of meanness and hatred, so Hiram didn't take a lot of stock in her affection for him.

In San Francisco, taxis were often waiting by the train station. Buggy drivers who would take you anywhere you wanted within the city, for a fee. But here, in Jubilee, Hiram glanced up and down the street and saw none.

A porter was scurrying by, a young man who looked scarcely old enough to shave.

"Excuse me, young man," Hiram said.

The porter stopped. "Yes sir?"

"I would like to find a taxi who could take me to the livery, where I might rent a buggy."

The porter shrugged his shoulders with a sheepish grin. "Ain't no taxis in this town, sir. This ain't the big city. But the livery is just a few blocks down the street."

Hiram was a little appalled that he was expected to walk. If the people of this town wanted his business, he expected them to show a little courtesy.

"Thank you," he said to the porter, and handed

him two bits.

The boy broke into a big smile. "Thank you, sir."

Hiram began his walk down the stretch of wooden boardwalks to the livery. The boards creaked underfoot in places, and one time he had to step down from the boardwalk to cross the front of an alley, and he found himself walking through mud an inch deep. When he stepped onto the next boardwalk, his once shiny shoes were now desecrated with mud.

He couldn't imagine why his boss wanted him to come to this town. The fact that his father lived in a nearby valley and his brother was the town marshal didn't seem relevant to him.

Officially, Hiram's boss wasn't really his boss. They were business partners, owning fifty-fifty in the various ventures they shared, but his partner had a reputation. The man's name was Aloysius Randall, and people who stood against him seemed to either die young or simply disappear. Even though they were officially partners, when Randall said to do something, Hiram did it.

Hiram had been a little reluctant to enter into business with him, but the potential to make money was too good to refuse. Indeed, over the past two years, Hiram had seen his net worth increase by a full third.

All Hiram knew about Randall's interest in this area was that Randall had tried to purchase the McCabe ranch more than once, and he had been refused every time.

Hiram had been in Randall's office when they discussed it.

Hiram had a glass of scotch in one hand. "Johnny McCabe sold most of his land to the government. From what I hear, the government is setting up some sort of Indian reservation. That land no longer has any value to me. There is no possible way the government would sell you that acreage, unless maybe you agreed to pay much more than the going rate. And there's no point in that. But the remaining acreage and the house would be of use. I plan to invest in mining in that area and the house would be a good base of operations for us."

Randall also held a glass of scotch, and he took a sip. "I plan to beat Johnny McCabe, and that blasted daughter of his. Her name is Sabrina and they call her Bree. How incredibly quaint." Randall shuddered. "They think they have beaten me, but they haven't."

Hiram wasn't sure what to think. "How do you plan to beat them?"

"That's for me to figure out."

"But, Aloysius, there's no profit in it. That ranch is off in a remote corner of the West."

Randall looked at him. "My motivations are my own."

And that was all he said on the matter.

So here Hiram was, in Jubilee, Montana. A small town on the edge of nowhere, with streets of mud and no taxis, and most of the men he saw on the street looked to be either miners or cowhands.

His job was to get two hotel rooms and then wait for Randall. But Randall had said it would be at least a few days before he arrived, so Hiram had a little time to kill.

At the livery, he rented a buggy and a horse. He climbed up onto the seat and took the reins in his hand, then he looked at the attendant. "I'm looking for the home of Matt McCabe. Could you give me directions?"

The attendant had a white beard and a tattered hat. He gave a slow, lazy shrug of his shoulders. "Could, but it won't do you no good."

Hiram was growing impatient. "And why, pray-tell, not?"

"Because that there buggy you rented won't get you there. He lives half way up a ridge. The ridge that's just east of town. About a quarter mile up Willbury Road, you'll see a small trail that breaks off to the right. Follow that trail about halfway up the ridge, and you'll find his place. But that buggy you just rented won't make it. The suspension is too delicate. You need a buckboard, or even better, a saddle horse."

"Then I would like to trade in this buggy for a buckboard."

The old-timer gave another slow shrug. "Cain't. Ain't none for rent. Folks around here own buckboards and use 'em for farm work or ranchin', but they don't rent 'em."

Hiram was losing his patience. "Then get me a horse."

The old-timer scratched his beard. "I don't know but that's a good idea. You know anything about riding?"

Hiram drew a breath, trying to steady his temper. It was like this old-timer was just prodding him to see his reaction. "Believe me, my father made sure all his sons could ride. Now are you going to waste my time here all day, or trade me the buggy for a horse that can climb that ridge?"

The old man shrugged his shoulders again. "Don't have to be so t'echy."

He went to the corral out behind the livery and dropped a loop on a roan. "Want me to saddle him for you? Hate to see your nice suit get all dirty."

"No. I don't want to be here all day listening to you blather. I'll do it myself."

The old man watched as Hiram saddled the horse. "I gotta say this for you, you might have soft, lily white hands, but you've saddled a horse before."

Hiram tied his carpet bag to the back of the saddle, then he swung up and onto the back of the horse.

The old man shook his head. "Ain't none of my business, but..."

Hiram closed his eyes with defeat. "What?"

"You're gonna be riding that there horse up the side of a ridge. Through stands of pine and alder."

"What about it?"

"You look like you're in your Sunday-go-to-meetin' clothes. Them duds ain't gonna stand up to that kind of treatment."

"Then what would you recommend?"

"I'd recommend Franklin's, down the street."

Hiram didn't know if he believed God existed. But if God did indeed exist, Hiram knew that God was laughing at him right now. "And what, might I ask, is Franklin's?"

"Franklin's Mercantile. Best place to buy the kind of clothes you need for the ride ahead of you. Started up by Charlie Franklin, one of the first citizens of this town. Except he don't run it no more. Run by May McCabe."

"McCabe?"

The old man nodded his head. "Daughter of Johnny McCabe hisself." The old man scratched his beard. "Except she's gotten married. Don't think her name's McCabe anymore. Don't know that it ever was, now that I think about it. Old Johnny's family is kind of hard to keep track of."

Hiram had had enough. He turned the horse away from the livery and rode on down the street.

2

HIRAM STEPPED OUT of the small dressing room at Franklin's, and he now wore jeans and a new range shirt. On his feet were black riding boots.

A girl who couldn't have been much older than twelve stood by the counter. "I don't know, Mister. You still look like a city slicker to me."

May was behind the counter. "Tildy!"

Tildy shrugged. "Well, he does."

The clothes Hiram had arrived in were rolled up and tucked under one arm. He hesitated a moment at the counter, considering the ride ahead of him. The small revolver that was still in his jacket might not be sufficient. His gaze fell on five revolvers on a shelf behind the counter.

"I presume those pistols are for sale?"

May nodded her head. "Yes, sir."

"I would like to see the one on the left."

May fetched it for him.

He spun the cylinder, making sure it was empty.

Tildy said, "That's a Colt forty-four."

"I know what it is."

"Actually, it's a forty-four forty. Takes the same cartridges that a lot of Winchester rifles do. That way you only have to carry one type of cartridge in your gunbelt."

What was it with the people in this town? "I *know* what it is."

He said to May, "I'll take it. And a box of ammunition."

Tildy was grinning at him. "You need a gunbelt, too."

May gave her a look. "Tildy..."

"What? He's got a horse outside and he's bought clothes to dress like a cowhand. He's gonna go riding. You buy a gun like that, you need a holster to put it in."

She looked at Hiram. "You know why men who

ride horses a lot carry a pistol?"

He was growing weary. "Yes."

"It ain't to shoot Indians an' outlaws. Though all the dime novels would make you think otherwise."

"I know."

"It's so if their horse throws them and their foot gets caught in the stirrup, they can shoot the horse and not get dragged to death."

"How could I possibly grow up, the son of Matt McCabe, and not know those things?"

Tildy's mouth fell open. "You're the son of Matt McCabe? That makes me your cousin. Well, kind of. Johnny McCabe is kind of my father." She glanced at May. "Well, *our* father. We have another father, too, but Johnny is kind of our father. Well, he's May's real father. That makes me your cousin. Kind of."

Hiram was aggravated with himself. He hadn't intended to reveal his identity any more than was necessary. "Are you ever quiet?"

May grinned. "When she's asleep. I'm sorry. She runs off at the mouth."

Tildy was looking at him. "Is Matt McCabe really your father? That means you must be Hiram."

Hiram produced a wallet from his jeans pocket. "That's what they tell me."

He paid May. "Keep the change."

Tildy said, "But you still need a gunbelt. And a hat. That sun will cook your brains if you try to ride all the way to Uncle Matt's on a hot day like this with that little hat you came in here with."

Hiram left the store with his old clothes tucked under one arm, a new Boss of the Plains hat pulled down over his temples, and a gunbelt buckled about his hips.

"Wow," Tildy said to May. "Can you believe it? He's our cousin. Didn't seem too friendly, though."

"Tildy, you have to learn not to talk so fast or so much."

"But look at all that stuff I sold him."

May came out from behind the counter and went to a front window. She watched as Hiram McCabe tucked his rolled up suit into the carpet bag tied to the back of his saddle. Then he mounted up and rode off down the street. For a city slicker, he looked natural in the saddle. May figured it was probably that way with all McCabe men.

Tildy wasn't sure what her sister was doing. "Wat'cha looking out the window for?"

May had heard the stories about Hiram, though she had kept them from Tildy. What could he be doing here in town?

Heck stepped in from the back door. He had been splitting firewood. They would need it tonight—it was early June and the days were warm with early summer, but the nights still got downright cold. "What're you doing, May?"

Tildy said, "She's watching our new cousin ride away."

May looked at Heck. "Hiram McCabe is in town."

That got Heck's attention. "What's he doing here?"

May shrugged. "He said he was here to see his father. Bought some clothes and a gun."

Tildy bounced on her toes. "I talked him into buying a gunbelt and a hat. Spends money like he's got it coming out of his ears."

Heck said to May, "Want me to run over to the marshal's office and tell Tom?"

She nodded her head. "Might be a good idea."

Tildy gave May a look, then she directed it at Heck. "All right. What are you two not telling me?"

3

TEN YEARS GO, Matt brought Peddie to this valley and they built a small cabin on a flat area, sort of a shelf, partway up the ridge. Within view of the cabin was a low point, almost a pass that looked like it had been cut along the summit of the ridge. Ride up and through that pass, and down the other side of the ridge, and you would be in the valley. Matt had made the journey so many times that he had worn a little trail up and through the pass. Another trail led down and away from the shelf, and to a road down below that would lead into town.

At one time, Matt had run one of the biggest ranches in California. Not quite as big as the Barkley Ranch outside of Stockton, but a close second. He had smoked fine cigars from Cuba, and he had conducted business from a mahogany desk in his study, often wearing a bolo tie and a pinstriped jacket. That was where he managed his empire. Though he hadn't been really managing it, he had learned over the years. His wife at the time, Verna, had been managing it the whole time. And she had been managing him, like a puppet on a string.

He thought about those days as he stood on the small porch in front of the cabin, a cup of coffee in one hand, looking up at the notched summit.

Matt had always been the tallest of his brothers, and he had the leanest build. Not that he wasn't strong, he just didn't look it.

He had taken to wearing a mustache during his years in California, when he had taken over the McCarty Ranch from Verna's father. Verna had said it made him look distinguished. He had shaved the mustache off when he left behind the ranch and that woman, and her crookedness and conniving. He thought he wanted a new beginning, and since he had ridden into California with only the clothes on his back and no mustache, and he was leaving California with the same amount of belongings, he would also do so without a mustache.

In recent years, he had grown it back and had grown a goatee to match. Peddie said he looked natural with whiskers.

It was mid-morning and he had already been working in the small garden where he grew crops for himself and Peddie. Corn, potatoes, tomatoes. A little rhubarb. Where he had at one time been one of the most successful ranchers in California, a man who was sometimes called a cattle baron, he was now content to work his small farm.

Most cattlemen looked with disdain on the work of a farmer, but Matt was finding contentment with it. It was the work he had learned on the family farm, back in Pennsylvania. He felt like, in a way, his life had gone full circle.

He no longer wore ties, or boots that cost more than a cowhand's pay for an entire year. He was in jeans that were faded, and he wore a flannel shirt. On his feet were riding boots—he had never gone back to the type of boots farmers often wore—but they were scratched and worn.

He and Peddie made little money. He would sometimes sell firewood to the farmers in the valley or to folks in town. He would trade with May, firewood for a sack of coffee or sugar, or a box of ammunition.

He was no expert with a gun like his brother Johnny, or Johnny's son Dusty. Even Matt's own son Tom was making a name for himself with a gun. But Matt could shoot straight enough, and like his brothers, he had the ability to remain strangely calm when bullets were flying. Must run in the family, he thought. But he had never been one for trick shooting.

When he wore a gun, it was a Smith & Wesson .38 caliber Model Three. Johnny, however, preferred the Colt. Said it was better balanced, and maybe it was for someone with Johnny's shooting skills. Dusty and Tom used Colts, too, but Matt was satisfied with his Smith and Wesson. He liked the feel of it in his hand, and the way you broke it open like a shotgun to load it, rather than loading it through a side loading gate.

Peddie stepped out from the kitchen with a kettle of coffee. Her sandy hair now showed streaks of silver and it was tied up into a bun behind her head.

"There's enough in here for one more cup, if you'd like."

He grinned. "I would never say no to another cup."

She began pouring. "You do drink a lot of coffee. But I never knew a cowhand who didn't."

He shrugged his shoulders. "But then, I'm not a cowhand anymore. I'm a farmer."

"You'll always be a cowhand at heart."

He grinned and took a sip.

She shook her head. "Haley told me that she told you to cut down on coffee. Too much isn't good."

He smiled. "First thing tomorrow."

He let his gaze drift back to the ridge and the notch.

She said, "You've been thinking about the old days, haven't you? Your life in California."

He nodded his head.

"I can tell when you have. There's something different about the look in your eyes."

He shrugged. "It's hard not to think about those times. I made a big mistake with Verna. It took a lot of years out of my life, years I won't get back."

"It was a long time ago. Look at the life you have now. And Tom and Danny are here with you."

Matt nodded. "It just haunts me sometimes."

"You're a good man, otherwise you wouldn't be bothered by it. But maybe you should look more at the man you are now and the life you're leading here."

He nodded his head and he looked at her with a grin. "I used to call Johnny morose, back in the old days. Looks like I've taken after him."

"Don't take after him too much." She turned to

head back into the kitchen, then she turned back toward him as a thought occurred to her. "Oh, don't forget, we've been invited to the ranch for supper tonight. It's been too long since we've seen everyone."

"That it has."

Peddie went back into the kitchen, and Matt returned his gaze to the wooded ridgeline. His thoughts were now on dinner at the ranch. He missed Temperance's cooking, now that she and Josh had moved to Wyoming. But Jessica's cooking was tasty.

It had been too long since they had seen Johnny and Jessica. And Aunt Ginny and Sam had been invited. Peddie had considered Jessica and Sam to be family long before Matt and Johnny had come into their lives.

Peddie came back out with a cup of tea in one hand. She stood beside him, and he reached one arm over her shoulders and pulled her in closer. That got a smile out of her.

He said, "Maybe it's because of those days in California that I appreciate you so much."

"I'll admit, I think about those days too. The hard years, before I met you. They come back on me at night, sometimes. I relive them in my dreams."

Before she could say anything else, something caught her attention. Movement, to the right and off a ways. "Matt, I think we have a rider coming."

He followed her gaze. His eyes weren't as good as they once were. He had taken to wearing spectacles at times, but he wondered if they really did any good.

"That's the trail that leads down to Willbury Road. We hardly ever get any riders from that direction. Usually from the valley. And it's usually Johnny or Dusty or Bree."

Then something struck him as familiar about the rider. The way a man sits in the saddle, moving with the horse as the horse steps along, can be as unique as the way a man walks. "No, it can't be."

"Who do you think it is?"

If the rider was who Matt thought he was, it was a man Matt had never expected to see again.

"Peddie, run inside and fetch my gunbelt."

4

HIRAM REINED UP in front of the porch of the little cabin. A man he could scarcely believe was his father stood on the front porch. His father had always dressed the part of a cattle baron in California, but now he looked like a cross between a farmer and a gunfighter.

Buckled about his hips was a gunbelt, not the one he had used in California, which had been ornate, with swirls carved into it and conchos on the holster. This was a simple belt with a holster that looked like it might have been Army surplus, with the top flap cut away. The man had a mustache and goatee that were nearly white.

Lines were carved into his face—lines Hiram didn't remember being there before.

"Father," Hiram said.

"Hiram? Is that really you?"

Hiram nodded. "Yes indeed."

"So, you're calling me *father*, again? The last time I saw you, you told me you weren't mine. You said your mother had said your father was that lackey of hers, Timmons, who used to follow her around like a dog."

Hiram nodded his head reluctantly. "That's the way of it. But I grew up believing you were my father. I learned from you. I would hope I take some of that with me."

"What brings you to Montana? I can't believe you came all this way to tell me that."

Hiram shook his head. "I'm here on business. But while I was here, I thought I would take the time to visit you. Maybe reconnect with you."

"What do you do for business these days?"

"I have partnered up with a man who has interest in shipping companies, banking and land speculation."

"What's his name?"

Hiram found himself a little reluctant to give it. "Aloysius Randall."

Matt shook his head. "The apple doesn't fall far

from the tree, does it? Your mother's tree. Maybe it's best that you just ride away."

"But father..."

"I meant what I said, the last time we talked. At least part of the blame for how you turned out is mine. Maybe most of it. I should have stood tough. I should have insisted on helping raise you, like I did with Tom and Danny. But your mother wanted to do most of it and, when it came to her, for far too long I saw what I wanted to see and not what was really there. And you're the victim in all of it."

"May I get down from this horse? Maybe have a cup of coffee with you?"

Matt shook his head. "Why else are you here? Everything your mother did was with a dual agenda, and you learned well from her."

Hiram shrugged his shoulders and looked a little sheepish. "Well, one piece of land I'm here to research is Uncle Johnny's ranch. Maybe make an offer for it. I was hoping you could arrange a meeting between us. Maybe put in a good word for me."

Matt gave a weary sigh. "Maybe it would be best if you just turned your horse around and rode back to town."

"Father, the remaining acreage and the house itself are worth a fair amount of money, and Aloysius is willing to pay above market value. He wants the house to serve as our base of operations in the area. We intend to buy into some of the mines here. It would behoove Uncle Johnny to hear my offer."

"I'm not gonna say it again."

Hiram gave a long look at Matt, then he tugged on the reins to turn the horse, and he rode away.

Matt had asked Peddie to wait inside after she brought the gunbelt. She stood just inside the kitchen with the door ajar and, as Hiram rode away, she stepped back outside. "I know it's hard, seeing him and the man he turned out to be. Are you all right?"

Matt's gaze was on Hiram as he worked his way

down the trail, back toward town. "As much as I ever will be."

5

TOM McCABE SAT at his desk with a stack of reward fliers in front of him. He was in a white shirt and a string tie, and the town marshal's badge was pinned to his left shirt pocket.

Each one of the fliers had to be read, and then he would decide which ones to post. He reached up to rub his tired eyes. Dang, but he hated paperwork.

Danny stood at the stove, pouring the last of a kettle of coffee into a cup. Tom figured the coffee had gone cold because the fire in the stove had long gone out. He had made the coffee earlier in the morning, before the heat of the day and the stove could combine to turn the office into an oven.

Danny had been little more than a boy when he and Tom had left California with their father and their Uncle Johnny. Now he had filled out, mostly with muscle but a little bit of a pot belly was starting to form. Too many of those good-tasting dinners at the Second Chance, Tom figured. Danny had a deputy's badge pinned to his shirt and a gunbelt was buckled about his hips.

Some law enforcement agencies west of the Missouri were starting to wear uniforms, like the constables of St. Louis and San Francisco, but Tom thought it would be a while before the Town Council ponied up the money for uniforms in Jubilee. He was more than happy not to wear one, anyway.

Danny set the empty kettle back on the stove. "Hey, Tom. It's ten o'clock. Want me to go walk the rounds?"

It was Tuesday morning. As chaotic as this town could become on a Saturday night when the cowhands and miners got paid, on a weekday morning the pace was sleepy and slow. Just the way Tom liked it.

He pushed away from his desk. "No, I think I'll go walk 'em myself. I've had about enough paperwork. Need to rest my eyes. This job has more paperwork than

I ever saw as a minister."

Danny grinned. "Least you don't have to wear that collar no more."

Tom buckled on his gunbelt. "'Sides, you've got your coffee to finish."

Danny held up his cup. "Right. It's good to have priorities."

"Hold down the fort, will you?" Tom grabbed his hat and headed for the door.

"Sure thing, Boss."

Tom stopped in the doorway and looked back at his brother. "If you get bored, don't be afraid to start going through those reward fliers. Only got about fifty of 'em in that stack."

"What? Couldn't hear you."

Tom grinned. "Right."

He stepped out onto the boardwalk.

On a Saturday afternoon, when the miners and cowhands got their monthly pay, Tom would walk the rounds with a scattergun to show he meant business. But on a sleepy morning like this one, the Colt Peacemaker in his holster would suffice.

He thought once his rounds were finished, he might stop in at the small house he and Hilly owned, over on Third Street.

He had married Hilly three years ago. They had an anniversary coming up in a couple of months and he wanted to do something special for it, but he didn't know what he could do on a marshal's salary.

He had been married years ago to a woman by the name of Leticia, but he had called her Lettie. She had been happy as the wife of a Methodist minister—but not as the wife of a lawman. She was honest enough with herself to admit she had married the profession and not the man, but that didn't make the divorce any easier on their daughter Mercy.

As a Christian, Tom didn't believe in divorce. Even more, since he had been a minister when he first came to this town, he thought he had to set an example. And yet, he had signed the divorce papers.

He was surprised at how little he felt when he signed them. Apparently his love for her had been fading without him even being aware of it.

He was even more surprised that, when Lettie left for Ohio to live with her mother, she didn't want to take Mercy with her.

Lettie had said she intended to have Christmas with Mercy, if the trails were open. The railroad hadn't yet reached Jubilee and, as Tom had expected, the trails were closed by November with the heavy snowfall that got dropped on them in the mountains of Montana.

Lettie then wrote that she would instead be in town for Mercy's birthday in June. Turned out she didn't do that, either. An aunt was sick in Ohio and Lettie said she was needed there.

At first, Lettie wrote long letters to Mercy. Because Mercy had been young and couldn't yet read cursive handwriting, Tom read them to her. Letters filled with a mother's love—a mother who missed her daughter. As time passed, the letters became fewer and shorter. Mercy now received maybe one or two a year. And she had not seen her mother since the day her mother boarded a stagecoach to head for Ohio.

Hilly had come into their lives a few months after Lettie left. Hilly was the new school marm, who didn't look the way Tom remembered school marms looking when he was a kid. Blue eyes, hair the color of straw. A smile that stopped him cold and made him forget to breathe.

Hilly had stolen Tom's heart the first time he looked at her, and it wasn't long before she was spending evenings with Tom and Mercy. Joining their lives like she belonged there.

One day, Mercy said to him, "Pa, when you gonna ask Miss Hilly to marry you?"

It was over breakfast, and it caught him a little off guard. "Well, such things have to be thought about long in advance. And you have to know the woman really well before you can ask her something like that."

"Well, Pa, you wait too long and someone else might come along and snatch her up."

"Oh, Mercy, I don't think that'll happen."

She shrugged her shoulders. "I don't know. She's a real winner."

That evening, he asked Hilly to marry him.

Mercy was growing up faster than he thought was possible. Every morning, he expected an eight year to come out of her bedroom, but the girl who emerged was fifteen.

A young man who worked at the assayer's office had taken a shine to her, and they had shared more than one dance at a shindig a few weeks ago.

During a waltz, Tom had thought they were dancing too close together and was about to intervene when Hilly put a hand on his arm.

"Leave it be. They're fine. She's a young woman, now."

That night, as Tom finally got to stretch out in bed and let his head sink into the pillow, he thought about how Hilly had taken over much of the role of Mercy's mother.

"I'm grateful for you, you know that? You have stepped in, filling Lettie's shoes. That was never required."

"Any child of yours is a child of mine."

"You have made such a difference in her life. I want you to know that. You have in my life too, but the good you have done her goes beyond words."

He could tell she was smiling by the way she formed her words. "You have both brought so much to my life, too."

He found he was also smiling. "Maybe that's the way it's meant to work."

All of this was running through Tom's mind as he stepped along the boardwalk. His heels thunked along on the boards underfoot and his spurs jingled a little with each step.

The town was made up mostly of buildings that had been slapped together in a hurry with two-by-fours and planks, like with most boom towns. Some of the rooflines were a little uneven, and more than one window wasn't lined up quite right.

Some boom towns faded after a while, but others had longevity, and Tom thought Jubilee was showing itself to be in the second group.

A train station had been built of brick and mortar—the railroad company intended for the station to be here for a while. Across from Tom's office had been a ramshackle structure that served as home to an oddities and trinkets shop. The building had been taken down and a new one was going up that had a solid foundation of granite slabs, and it also had brick siding.

The bank in town was now also a solid building, and it had a steel vault that had been shipped out all the way from St. Louis.

All signs that Jubilee was growing from a boom town into a community that would stand for years.

As Tom walked along, he heard the call of the morning train. When he got to the train station, he glanced at the small crowd on the platform. Some folks arriving and others getting ready to board.

One man stepped down from the platform to the boardwalk. He looked to be about thirty and had long hair and a neatly trimmed goatee, and a long dark gray duster coat. Tom knew the man, though the last time Tom had seen him, the man's beard had looked like a wild growing bush and there had been nothing neatly trimmed about him.

"Gabe Quint, if I'm not mistaken."

The man squinted his eyes as he looked at Tom from under a black, wide-brimmed hat with a flat crown. "Why, Sheriff McCabe. I heard you were still running things, up here in Jubilee."

Quint had a carpet bag in one hand, and the other held a double barrel shotgun.

Tom said, "Last time I saw you, I told you to leave

town or you'd be facing thirty days in jail. That's what Judge Mack decided."

Quint shook his head. "That old whiskey-swilling judge don't scare me none. Besides, I'm here on business. The company I work for sent me."

Tom didn't find this man amusing at all. "That a fact."

"Yes, indeed."

"How long you planning to stay?"

"Long as I need to, to get the job done."

Quint moved to step around Tom, and Tom side-stepped into his way. "And what might that job be?"

"Land acquisition. I'm a land speculator. Or, at least, I work for one."

Tom chuckled. "You? A land speculator? You're a back-shooting gun for hire. Can you even sign your name?"

"Get out of my way, McCabe. I ain't broke no laws."

"You got involved in a saloon brawl at the Second Chance that turned into a shooting match. You killed two men."

"They was shootin' at me. Besides, you said there would be no charges filed ag'in me if I left town."

"I said if you left town and didn't come back."

"All right, then arrest me. That incident was almost four years ago. Doubt there's anyone left here in town who could serve as a witness."

"Hunter, the saloon owner."

"Them charges won't stick. The company I work for has got good lawyers and lots of money."

"And who do you work for?"

"Singleton Property Development. Ever heard of us?"

Tom had to think for a moment. The name sounded familiar but he wasn't sure where he had heard it.

Quint looked at him. "Now who's the stupid one? They're only fast becoming the biggest land company in

California. Spreading their wings a bit, into Texas and all the way up here to Montana." Quint grinned. "Now, if you ain't gonna arrest me, get out of my way."

Tom knew Quint was right. The only witness was Hunter, and Hunter had admitted he wasn't quite sure what he had seen. It had all happened so fast. Hunter thought Quint had fired first, but he wouldn't stake his life on it.

At the time, Judge Mack had said to him, in a whiskey-soaked voice, "The most we could get on Quint is disorderly conduct. Thirty days in the town jail."

"Is that what you get for disorderly conduct?" Tom said.

The judge shrugged his shoulders. "Ain't gonna go look it up now. Go tell him thirty days."

Tom hesitated. He rested his hands on his hips. "Well, Judge, with all due respect, I don't like the idea of the town paying for thirty days' worth of meals for him. The town budget is kind of small."

"All right. Then tell him if he rides away and don't come back, we won't file any charges."

Tom stepped aside so Quint could move along.

"Thank you kindly, Sheriff," Quint grinned again and continued walking along.

Tom was about to tell him it wasn't *sheriff*, it was *marshal*, but he figured why bother?

He watched as Quint strolled his way down the boardwalk and then turned into the hotel that was called the Randall House and stepped up onto their front porch.

Tom made a mental note to tell Danny to keep an eye on that man.

This was shaping up to be a strange week, he thought. First Hiram had arrived this morning—not that Tom had seen him, but he accepted the word of May and Heck. And now Gabe Quint was back in town.

He began walking again, continuing his rounds. The train station was on Randall Street, which would become Randall Road if it was followed far enough outside of town.

Just ahead of him, on his right, was Third Street, where his house was. After a cup of coffee with Hilly, he would head back down to Main Street.

He noticed a rider approaching along Randall. "Speak of the devil," he muttered.

The man had gray hair that fell to his shoulders, and a wild beard. Pulled down over his head was a worn, wide-brimmed hat that was a neutral gray. He was in a range shirt and the new jeans many cowhands were now wearing. A revolver rode at his right hip, and another was tucked into the front of his gunbelt.

"Howdy-do, Marshal," the man called out.

"Judge Mack. Didn't expect to see you for a while."

Mack was the circuit judge, and he wasn't due in town for another six weeks.

"I had nothin' on the docket so I figured I'd ride out here and spend time with my sweet Angie."

Tom couldn't help but grin.

Judge Mack's face was crisscrossed with lines that were carved deep. He spoke like an old scout who had downed too much whiskey and breathed too much campfire smoke over the years. That was how he looked, too.

The judge squinted at him. "Maybe after I visit with Angie a while, I'll swing on down to the Second Chance and let you buy me a drink."

Tom nodded. "You do that."

6

HIRAM BOUGHT a bottle of whiskey at the bar in the hotel, and he went up to his room and poured himself a glass. It was only a little after twelve, kind of early to start drinking, but he figured he had a good enough reason, considering the way the visit with his father had gone.

He unbuckled his gunbelt and looped it over the back of a chair. Then he sat at the edge of the bed with the glass of whiskey in one hand, and he let the exchange between him and the man he called his father roll over in his mind.

He didn't think he should care what Matt McCabe thought of him. But for some reason he did.

Hiram had been raised by Mother to be independent. To survive. And you can't do that if you're concerned about what other people think of you. When his father and Tom and Danny had left for Montana, Hiram decided not to care. When Mother died, it left Hiram alone in the world, but again, he decided not to care. Mother had raised him to need no one but himself.

The last time he had seen Tom was when Tom had threatened to kill him if he ever put Tom's family in danger again. Hiram hadn't been sure what his brother was talking about, but he knew more than one cutthroat had been working for Mother, and she tended to see that things that were necessary got done. Hiram figured she had done something to threaten Tom or his family, and Tom thought the threat had come from Hiram.

Tom had stood in front of him, a Methodist minister but not wearing a collar that day. He had a gun strapped to his hip.

Tom had said, "If you ever interfere in our lives again, I'll find you and put a bullet in your head."

Not what Hiram expected to hear from him. "I thought you were a man of God."

"I am. But sometimes even a man of God has to make a stand. You forced me into it when those men attacked. Make no mistake, I'll put a bullet in you and not lose any sleep over it."

Those were the last words Tom had ever said to him. Hiram had heard over the years that his brother had left the ministry and become a lawman. Hiram wasn't surprised. Tom had McCabe blood. It showed in the look in his eyes and the determination in his steps when he walked.

Hiram had to admit to feeling a little envy. He had the name, but it wasn't enough. He sometimes found himself wishing he had McCabe blood flowing through his own veins.

And then there was his younger brother Danny. Hiram actually didn't remember the last time he had seen Danny. What Danny's last words to him were.

Mother would have said Hiram was being weak. All he should need was himself.

He took a belt of whiskey, wanting it to wash away the pain he wished wasn't there. It didn't.

There was a knock at the door. Either room service, he figured, or Randall was here a few days earlier than planned.

He got to his feet and walked over to the door, his glass in one hand, and he slid open the dead bolt and pulled the door open.

The man in the doorway wasn't who he expected.

"Gabe Quint," Hiram said.

"Mister Randall ain't comin'." Quint pushed past him. "Sent me instead."

"I rented him a room. It's the next door down."

Quint nodded. "I'll be takin' it. Have you seen Judge Mack, yet?"

"I didn't know he was in town."

Quint dropped his carpet bag and went over to the chest of drawers where the whiskey bottle stood. "Mister Randall figured he'll be here soon, if he ain't already. There's some saloon whore in town the judge has taken a shine to. He comes here a lot when he's not in court."

"How does Aloysius know these things?"

"Keeps his ear to the ground. Pays attention. Wouldn't hurt for you to start doing that." A second glass waited by the bottle, and Quint filled it with whiskey to the halfway point. "Between you and me, I don't know why he keeps you around. You ain't good for much. Makes some of his businesses look legit, I suppose."

Quint took down a mouthful of the whiskey.

"Mister Quint, I would thank you to leave. Your room is down the hall."

Quint grinned. "I suppose you would."

"I have to ask. Do you know what Aloysius's business is with the judge?"

Quint was still grinning. "He didn't tell you?"

Hiram shook his head.

"We have to remove him from his position as judge. Once he's gone, I'll send word to Mister Randall. He will then contact the Territorial Governor, a friend of his, and one of Mister Randall's men will find himself appointed as the new judge."

"And how are we to remove the judge from the bench?"

Quint was still grinning, and he slapped the side of his holster. "That's what he sent me along for."

Hiram blinked with surprise. "You're going to shoot him?"

Quint shrugged his shoulders. "Seems a quick way to take care of the problem."

"But...you can't just shoot him."

"Why not?"

Hiram was flabbergasted. "There are laws."

"Out here?" Quint took another chug of whiskey and waited a moment while it burned its way down. "Out here, city slicker, there ain't a whole lot of law. You catch a man on the trail and put a bullet in him, might be a day or two before anyone finds him. And that's if the wolves don't find him first. They'll never know who did it."

Hiram didn't know if he was more appalled at Quint's casual attitude for murder, or Quint's belief that he could get away with it so easily. "But how can you know for sure?"

Quint shrugged again. "It's what I do for a living. Why do you think Mister Randall keeps me around?"

Hiram found himself spontaneously taking a step backward. This was a lot to take in. "What could possibly be gained from all of that? I understood we were here to acquire some new property. Buy interest in at least one of the mines."

"And to acquire the McCabe Ranch."

Hiram nodded his head. "That's right."

"What Mister Randall ain't told you is he doesn't just want the ranch. He wants to crush Johnny McCabe in the process. Maybe put a bullet in him, though I ain't too confident in that part of it. Too many men have tried over the years, and they're all in the ground. And his sons are all gunfighters. They say the one called Dusty is even better'n he is."

"But why?"

Quint took down the remainder of the whiskey in his glass. "I prob'ly shouldn't say this, but you'd find out sooner or later. Mister Randall likes 'em young. Girls, I mean. And he don't take *no* for an answer. He took a liking to McCabe's daughter, and when she said *no*, he tried to teach her that you don't do that. But he didn't take into account that she's a McCabe. She beat him almost unconscious."

Hiram was just standing and staring at Quint. He realized he wasn't breathing so he forced himself to inhale.

Quint chuckled. "Kind of funny, being beaten up by a girl. But this ain't just any girl. It's Johnny McCabe's daughter. They say she's half wildcat. Mister Randall figured if he showed up here in town, either she would put a bullet in him or the old man himself would. They say the girl is a crack shot. They say she's as good as Annie Oakley."

"I'm not familiar with that name."

"Part of the Buffalo Bill Wild West show, started up about three years ago."

Hiram shook his head.

Quint said, "Don't matter none. Mister Randall sent me here to get the job done. And the first part of that job is removing Judge Mack."

Hiram was feeling lightheaded, so he sat at the edge of the bed again.

Quint didn't seem to notice. "I'm hungry. Where can you grab a meal in this town?"

Hiram didn't want to eat at the Second Chance. That place had ties to the McCabe family, and Hiram found himself wanting to avoid those people as much as he could. He saw the look in his father's eyes, when his father looked at him. Hiram didn't want to see that in any of the others. But he was aware of another place. "A restaurant called the Cattleman's Club, further up Main Street. I'm not sure when they open, but the clerk at the desk downstairs said the food's quite good."

"I'll take my things to my room and I'll be back in a couple of minutes, and we can both go. You're buying." He grabbed the bottle of whiskey. "I'll take this. It's a man's drink. Too much for the likes of you."

7

STOCKYARDS HAD BEEN BUILT outside of Jubilee. The train would first stop in town at the station to let passengers deboard and new passengers climb on, and then it would chug its way slowly to the stockyards outside of town where it would stop again, and passengers would have to wait patiently while cattle were removed from the stock cars or loaded onto them.

Johnny McCabe sat in the saddle atop a small, grassy hill, looking down at the pens that were filled with reddish brown cows with no horns.

Dusty had reined up beside him and was leaning one elbow on the saddle horn. "Is that Red Angus, Pa?"

Johnny nodded his head. "So I'm told."

Charles was with them. "Looks like about eighty head."

"Should be." They had purchased sixty steers, twenty cows and two bulls.

Dusty nodded his head. "Should be plenty to rebuild the herd with."

Johnny had a little uncertainty in his voice. "They aren't Longhorns, but I guess they'll do."

They had bought these from the ranch Josh now worked for as the ramrod. The Bar V, outside of Medicine Bow. Johnny knew little about the new breeds of cattle, and since Josh worked with Red Angus and Johnny thought there were few who knew more about cattle than Josh did, he decided to go with Red Angus as the breed to rebuild the McCabe herd with. And, he thought, why not buy the cattle from Josh himself?

"Look at them short, little legs," Dusty said. "Are you sure they can handle even the three miles from here to the ranch?"

Johnny shook his head. "I'm not sure of anything. Josh says they can hold up to a short cattle drive, as long as we don't push 'em too hard. Or too fast."

They moved the small herd along Willbury Road at not much more than a walking pace. One steer turned away from the herd and took on the notion that he was going to head into a stand of pines, but Johnny's horse could outrun the critter easily, and Johnny turned the steer back to the herd.

These cows had more beef on the hoof than a Longhorn. Josh had said that was one of the benefits of the newer breeds of cattle and Johnny agreed.

It was one thing to observe some cows in Josh's pasture down in Wyoming, but it was another to ride along with the animals as they worked their way down Willbury Road. This gave Johnny a chance to see the cows up close. To get a feel for their disposition. He found that while they couldn't run with the same speed as a Longhorn, they were powerful creatures and could run well enough to trample a man if they were of a mind to, and the man got careless.

These critters couldn't run like a Longhorn so open range wouldn't be right for them. Instead, ranchers kept them in pastures, which meant Johnny, Dusty and Charles would be building fences.

He and the boys had spent the spring months cutting thick poles to serve as fence posts. They had marked off two separate pastures that were more than two hundred acres each. The original goal was to have one large pasture, but Johnny decided if one section of fence should come down, he didn't want the entire herd running loose. As the herd multiplied, he and the boys would build additional pastures as necessary.

Using posthole diggers, he and the boys had set about laying fence a month ago. He bought some rolls of barbed wire from May, and they began nailing strands of it to the posts, in place of fence rails.

At one point, Charles had straightened from his work, with a hammer in one hand, and he pulled off his hat and wiped away some sweat from his forehead. "I feel like a danged farmer."

Dusty grinned. "You look like a danged farmer,

too."

Johnny couldn't help but grin at the boys. "Something Mister Chen was trying to teach me, those last few days of his life. Times change. We've got to change with them, if we're gonna survive. It doesn't mean we change who we are. It just means we change how we do a few things."

Dusty's grin hadn't faded. "I still say Charles looks like a farmer."

Charles swatted him with his hat.

Johnny grinned at the memory as he and the boys moved the herd along, turning it toward the right and through the pass still known as McCabe Gap, and into the valley.

Johnny was riding a gray colored horse he called Ash. The horse was the son of Thunder. The horse had been nearly a solid gray when Thunder first brought him to Johnny as a young colt, but as Ash grew, his coat grew a little dappled.

Johnny had trained Ash using the way of the Shoshone. He found Ash a little less ornery than Thunder, but the horse had plenty of gumption and he was smart. Though not quite a cutting horse, Ash quickly got with the rhythm of the short cattle drive. When a second cow decided to bolt, Ash started moving before Johnny could direct him to, and as they cut off the animal, Johnny just held the reins loose while Ash drove the cow back to the herd.

Thunder wasn't really old by horse standards. Johnny had figured Thunder to be maybe four or five when the horse joined the family—that's how Johnny thought of it—and he still could be ridden. However, Thunder had cracked a hoof a few years ago, attacking a man who had shot Johnny. Thunder had saved Johnny's life, but he had developed as bad a crack in one hoof as Johnny had ever seen. With a braced up horse shoe, Johnny was able to ride him home, but Johnny figured it was that ride that had damaged the hoof beyond repair. The crack had healed, but Johnny didn't think it was strong enough to sustain the weight of a rider for very long.

A trail folks called McCabe Road cut south along the valley floor and led from the Gap to the McCabe Ranch headquarters. One pasture was within sight of the house, just beyond the small river that was spanned by a wooden bridge. Johnny and the boys had built a gate in the pasture by building a large, rectangular frame and bracing it with an X pattern, and it was held in place against a fence post by thick strips of leather that served as hinges.

The gate was open, and this was what they were driving the cattle toward.

Johnny saw a rider near the gate. As they drew closer, he could see it was Bree. She was in jeans, like a cowhand, and a gunbelt was buckled about her hips. She had positioned herself so that if the cattle didn't turn into the pasture through the gate, she would be directly in their path and could turn them toward the gate.

He hadn't asked her to be there, but she was solving a problem he had been wondering about. He had thought he might ride ahead of the herd and try to turn it, but now he wouldn't have to. As the herd approached her, she pulled the Stetson from her head and began waving it at the cattle and sent them through the open gate.

One steer tried to keep on going, but Bree was on a cutting horse and the horse knew what to do. It cut off the rogue steer and turned it back toward the gate.

Once the herd was in the pasture, Johnny sprang out of the saddle and swung the gate closed, and then he pulled a loop made of rope over one corner of the framework to hold the gate shut.

He looked at Bree. "Thanks for being here. You made the job a lot easier."

"I wanted to see the new herd arrive. This is a new era for this ranch."

Charles was smiling at her. "I knew I married the

right girl."

She gave him a smirk. "You're just figuring that out now?"

Johnny swung back up and into the saddle. "Let's leave the cows there for a while. Let 'em settle down and rest a bit. Get used to the new pasture and the new grass. In the morning, we'll move maybe forty of 'em over to the other pasture."

It was mid-afternoon. Moving this small herd from the stockyard outside of town to the pasture had taken a while. Dusty said, "I think I'll head on back to the house. See what Haley is fixing for supper."

Johnny nodded his head. "Matt and Peddie are coming over to the main house tonight. Aunt Ginny and Sam, too."

"Tell 'em all I said *hey.*"

8

JUDGE MACK SWUNG out of the saddle and gave the reins a couple of turns around the hitching rail. He intended to take his horse to the livery and pay the boy there to tend the animal, but not without seeing Angie first. It had been too long since he had seen her.

He knew he was too old for her—he wasn't kidding himself. But she seemed to like him regardless, and she made him feel young and alive. He had never been in love before he met her, and he wouldn't presume to have any claim to knowing what love was or what it felt like. But he figured it might feel something like how he felt for Angie.

The sign overhead read THE CATTLEMAN'S CLUB in swirly letters. Miss Alisha had forked over some cash to have the sign painted just right.

Judge Mack approached the front door and turned the knob but found it locked. He knew they opened at one o'clock in the afternoon, so he grabbed the chain of his pocket watch from a vest pocket, pulled the watch free and flipped it open. Still fifteen minutes to go before they opened.

He supposed he could take his horse down to the livery and, by the time he got back, the restaurant would be open. But he hadn't seen Angie in a couple of months and was just itching to look into those green eyes. So he slid the watch back into his pocket and then raised his knuckles and rapped on the door.

He waited a moment, and then he heard a woman's voice. "We're open in fifteen minutes."

Sounded like Angie.

He said, "Well, if you open this door, you'll get a big old hug and kiss."

He sure hoped it was Angie. If it was Miss Alisha or Miss Maybelle, then he had just embarrassed himself right good.

He could hear the latch sliding back and then the

door pulled open, and sure enough, it was Angie. She stood to his shoulders and had hair the color of straw, and it was all pulled back in a bun with a blue bandana tied down over it like a kerchief.

"Judge!" she called out and leaped at him, wrapping her arms around the back of his neck.

He pulled her in for a bear hug, lifting her feet from the floor and spinning her around. Their lips pressed against each other's like there was no tomorrow.

Maybelle stood by one of the tables. She was as tall as the Judge, with a long willowy neck and pronounced cheekbones, and skin the color of a chestnut. "Get in here, you two, before people start staring at you."

"Don't care if people stare at me," he said. "I got the most beautiful girl in the world right here and I don't care who knows it."

Maybelle couldn't help but smile. "It's good to see you, Judge. Angie has missed you something fierce."

"Good to see you too, Miss Maybelle." He set Angie back on the floor and followed her into the dining room. Maybelle shut the door and locked it again, and the Judge pulled Angie in for another kiss.

"What you doin' in town, Judge?" Angie said. "Didn't expect you for weeks."

"I had me a free docket, and I thought I'd spend some time with you."

Angie gave him a full smile. "I'm so glad you did."

"I've gotta go take my horse down to the livery. But then maybe, if Miss Alisha and Miss Maybelle don't mind, you can have the afternoon off. Got me a bottle of wine in my saddlebags, and it's just begging to be opened."

Maybelle grinned. "I don't mind, and I don't think Alisha will, either. Business is usually slow this time of the week. She's down at the Second Chance at the moment, having tea with Miss Ginny."

"Talking politics, I 'spect."

Maybelle nodded her head. "Most likely. They're both still on the Town Council."

Angie looked at the Judge. "You go take care of your horse. I must look a fright. Didn't know you were coming. I've gotta go upstairs and pretty myself up."

"You look beautiful to me right now, just as you are."

"Oh, Judge. You just say all the right things."

He winked at her. "That's 'cause I'm a judge."

She laughed.

He headed outside, and Angie scurried upstairs to her room. She was dismayed that the Judge saw her with her hair under a bandana, and just after she had scrubbed the floor in the kitchen. She wanted a long hot bath but there was no time for it. She would have to settle for a quick washing using a pitcher and basin, and then she would change into a nice dress.

She shut her bedroom door behind her and went to the mirror that was attached to the top of her dresser.

And then, in the mirror, she saw a man sitting on the edge of her bed.

She let out a yelp and turned to face him.

His face was scruffy and dirty with trail dust, and his shirt was stained from sweat and campfire smoke. Looked like a saddle bum, but he wore his gun like he knew how to use it. Most cowhands had a gun perched on the hip in a way that struck her as not looking quite natural, but this man's was at his left side and turned backward for a cross draw.

She realized she had seen him before. He had come into the Cattleman's Club the previous Saturday night and wanted a tumble with her. She told him she wasn't in that business anymore, that the Cattleman's was a legitimate establishment, and he would have to leave. But he had grabbed her hard by the shoulders and tried to force a kiss, which led to Angie crying out for help.

Alisha hit the man over the head with a bottle of bourbon, and while he was on his hands and knees trying to gather his senses, Maybelle called out the door for the marshal. Tom McCabe had just gone by, walking his rounds, and he came in and hauled the man to the town jail.

Afterward, Tom came back and said, "He's drunk. I don't know if his head will be hurting more from drinking or from you hitting him with that bottle."

Alisha said, "Serves him right."

"That it does. I'll hold him an extra day to drive home the point that I don't like women being handled rough in this town, then I'll send him on his way. Don't think he'll bother you anymore."

And yet, here he was, sitting on the edge of Angie's bed.

He said, "We've got some unfinished business, you and me."

"I told you before I ain't in that business no more."

"Don't matter to me none." He got to his feet.

She took a step backward. "Get out."

He shook his head. "Ain't going nowhere, not till I'm ready."

She ran for the door, but he was faster and cut her off.

She swung a hand at him, but he caught her by the wrist and pulled her in for a kiss.

She clawed at his face, leaving a row of bloody tracks along his cheekbone, and he shoved her away hard. She crashed into the window, her elbow breaking one pane of glass.

With one hand he wiped blood from the side of his face, and with the other he slid the bolt to lock the door. "You're gonna pay for that, you no good saloon trash."

Judge Mack stepped out the front door of the Cattleman's and said, "You're just the man I want to see."

Marvin Tucker was ambling along the boardwalk. Long and thin and with a perpetual smile on his face.

Mack knew the boy wasn't quite right, but he was harmless, and he worked well with horses.

"Judge Mack?" Marvin said, speaking slowly, like he wasn't quite accustomed to using words. "Didn't know you was back in town."

"That I am. You still work down at the livery?"

"Yessir. Me and Old Bob. We kind of run it together."

"I would appreciate it if you would take this horse down to the livery and see that he's taken care of." Mack dug into a vest pocket and handed Marvin a dime. "This is for you."

Marvin gave a big beaming smile at the sight of the dime. The coin nearly equaled a day's pay for him. "Thank you, sir."

"Let me get this first." Mack reached into a saddlebag and pulled out a bottle of white wine.

Then the window broke on the second floor of the Cattleman's. The pane cracked and a shard of glass fell to the ground.

Marvin squinted in the sunlight as he looked up at the window frame. "Wonder what caused that?"

"That's Angie's room!"

Maybelle hadn't locked the front door, and he charged back into the Cattleman's. With the bottle of wine in his hand now forgotten, he ran up the stairs.

Maybelle looked up from one table, where she was spreading out a table cloth. "Judge? What's wrong?"

The Judge stopped at Angie's door and then realized the bottle was still in his hand. He shifted the bottle to his left, then he turned the knob to find the door locked. "Angie?"

He heard her cry out from inside the room.

He knew all he needed to. His Angie was in some sort of trouble, and she needed him. He raised a foot and drove it into the door. The dead bolt gave way and the door flew open.

Angie was on the floor, hanging onto the side of her face, and a man stood over her. The Judge had seen enough in his life to know she had been struck.

The man had hold of her by one arm, and he looked at Mack. "Get out of here, old man."

"I ain't goin' nowhere. But you're gonna regret the day you was born."

The man let go of Angie's arm and pulled his revolver.

The Judge swung the bottle of wine toward the man and it caught him on the cheekbone. There were already some red streaks at the side of his face—the Judge figured Angie had clawed him but good.

The man recoiled back as the bottle broke apart across his face. Wine covered his face and spilled down to his shirt. He brought his hand up to cover a new set of cuts to go along with the streaks Angie had left on his cheekbone.

The Judge grabbed the man's gun hand and brought the wrist down over one knee, and the gun came loose from his grip.

Mack said, "Angie, are you all right?"

She was now sitting up, her back against the side of the bed. "I think so."

"Well, this jasper ain't gonna be."

The man tried to push past the Judge, but Mack grabbed him by the shirt, spun him around and drove a fist into his face.

The man landed against a dresser on one wall. Mack grabbed him by the shirt again and dragged him from the room. "Don't know who you are, boy, and I don't rightly care. You done made the mistake of a lifetime."

Mack brought him to the top of the stairs and gave him a shove.

Maybelle came running from the kitchen with a Colt Navy in her hands. At the sound of the commotion upstairs, and the sight of the Judge charging up there, she had run and grabbed the gun. She emerged from the kitchen to see a man somersaulting down the stairs. He landed on the floor at the foot of the stairs and was slow getting up.

"Judge," Maybelle said, looking up to the top of the stairs. "What's going on?"

"Found him in Angie's room, getting rough with her."

"How'd he get in here?"

"Don't know and don't rightly care. I'm pronouncin' judgement on him and it ain't gonna be good."

The Judge started down the stairs.

The man looked up at Maybelle. Blood streamed from cuts and scratches on his face, and she thought he looked like he had taken a punch to one eye.

He ran to her and gave her a backhand across the face, and he pulled the gun from her grip.

The Judge was now at the foot of the stairs.

The man cocked his gun and brought his arm out to full extension, aiming at the Judge. Mack had drawn his own revolver and pointed it at the man. Both guns went off at the same time.

The man's shot missed the Judge, the bullet tearing into the bannister. The Judge's shot didn't miss.

The bullet drove itself into the man's chest, and he staggered backward. The Judge fired again and the man went down.

Maybelle stood staring, wide-eyed. Her hands covered her mouth. Angie came running from her room to the top of the stairs to see the man fall backward from the Judge's second shot.

Maybelle then noticed two men had come in and stood in the open doorway, staring at what had just happened. She didn't know either of them.

Tom McCabe came running in, pushing past the men. His gun was in his hand, and Danny McCabe was behind him carrying a scattergun.

Tom glanced at the body on the floor, then to Judge Mack. The Judge's gun was still in his hand, smoke drifting from the barrel.

"We seen the whole thing, Marshal," one of the

men in the doorway said.

Tom looked at them. He realized one was his brother Hiram. The other was Gabe Quint.

Quint said, "The Judge shot that man down in cold blood. It was murder."

9

IN A TIME when most secretaries were men, Jack had hired a woman. Her name was Myrna, and she was twenty-two years old. She was dating Hector Hawley, Jack's sort-of brother. Her family was from New York City and had moved out a couple of years ago to find a fresh start.

She got the job when she and Hector had stepped into Jack's law office for a quick visit, and she had seen pieces of mail, dozens of it, strewn across the unoccupied desk in the front office. She took it upon herself to begin sorting mail, and when a potential client walked in, she grabbed the appointment book and penciled him in.

She said to Jack, "You need a secretary. When can I start?"

Jack shrugged his shoulders. "Right now?"

She looked at Hector, who had been planning to walk her home. "Can't walk home with you, Sweetie. I've gotta work."

Jack got criticized occasionally for having a female secretary, but Myrna organized the office like she was born to the job.

She spoke with a heavy New York accent, which made Jack grin sometimes. Instead of saying something like "the other thing," she would say "de uddah t'ing." And instead of "you guys," she would say, "Youse guys."

She tended to be a little bossy, but Hector said not to worry about it. "It's a New York thing. You'll get used to it."

And Jack found he did.

He came back into the office from the Second Chance on this sleepy weekday afternoon to find her at her desk, with a newspaper open. Such was to be expected on a day like this.

"Howdy, Myrna. Anyone come in while I was gone?"

"Nope. Nuttin' goin' on at all."

"That the morning paper?"

"Sure is, Sweetie. Fresh off the stage from Billings."

"Is the sports page there?"

She grinned and pulled off a back page and handed it to him.

The old baseball team he and his college buddy Darby Yates followed, the Boston Red Stockings, was playing well and a contender for the championship. Though now the Boston team was called the Beaneaters. Jack found it a little difficult getting accustomed to thinking of them as that.

He sat in the visitor's chair in front of Myrna's desk and glanced at the headlines.

He found what he was looking for. Boston had swept the Pittsburgh Alleghanies in a double header Saturday by scores of one to nothing and four to three.

When Jack and Darby had watched the games, back when they were in medical school in Boston, pitching had been done with an underhand toss. A *pitch*, like in horseshoes. But now it was done overhand, with the pitcher firing the ball into the catcher. There were two pitchers on the team who were among the best in the game, Old Hoss Radborne and John Clarkson.

Jack found he missed baseball and would love the chance to go to Boston and see those two pitchers. But as much as he liked baseball, going back to Boston would be difficult and too expensive.

That didn't mean he wasn't going to check the sports page every time a paper arrived from Billings, though. As of Saturday, the Boston team was now in first place, five and a half games ahead of the second place Cleveland Spiders. It was Tuesday, so Jack would have to wait a day or two more to get the results of Monday's game. There was no Sunday baseball in those days.

"You know, I think I might take the afternoon off

and go home. Spend some time with Nina."

Myrna nodded her head. "How far along is she?"

"Five months."

"Might be a good idea. When the Judge gets here in a few weeks, you'll be busy. But don't forget. You've got that will to draw up."

The will. That's right. He had forgotten about it. "I'll take it home and do it there. I'll need a witness, though."

"I can sign it in the morning."

That was what Jack wanted to hear. He got to his feet.

And then Danny McCabe came running in through the door, huffing for breath. "We need you down at the Cattleman's. There's been a shooting."

Myrna gave him a look of bored surprise. "On a Tuesday?"

Danny shrugged his shoulders. "You never know, I suppose."

Jack followed Danny to the Cattleman's, and that was when he discovered the Judge was already in town, but it looked like instead of presiding over a case of potential murder, he was going to be the defendant.

The Judge was sitting at a table, and Angie was with him. "It'll be all right, Judge. I know it will be."

A body was on floor, now covered with a sheet. Doc Martin said to Tom McCabe, "We need to find a couple of men to help get this body to my office, so I can write out a proper death certificate."

Doc Martin was the town coroner as well as the only doctor in town. Unless you counted Dusty's wife Haley, who was a folk doctor. What the old-timers called a granny woman or a granny doctor. But from what Jack had seen, he would trust Haley over Doc Martin when it came to treating most ailments.

"Judge, Angie," Jack said. "You both all right?"

Mack shrugged his shoulders. "We're fine. But that jasper what tried to get rough with Angie has seen better days."

Aunt Ginny was there, along with Alisha Summers. When they heard what happened, they left their tea at the Second Chance and hurried on over. And there were two men standing to one side. Men Jack had never seen before.

Tom said to Jack, referring to the men, "Before we go too far, you're gonna want to question these two. They claim to have seen the whole thing."

Gabe Quint placed his hands on his hips. "Ain't no *claim* about it a'tall, Marshal. We was standing by the door and seen the whole thing."

The other man rolled his eyes and looked a little embarrassed. He was in range clothes, but he wore them like a dandy. Like they were no more than a costume for him, rather than actual working clothes.

"That's Gabe Quint," Tom said. "And the other one is my brother Hiram."

Jack gave Hiram a long look. "So you're Hiram. I've heard a lot about you."

"Nothing good, I'm sure."

"To be honest, no."

Judge Mack looked up at Jack. "Don't know what you're doin' here, boy. Not like I can afford your rates."

"You need a lawyer."

He shrugged. "Need a lot of things."

"I'll take the case pro bono."

A man stepped through the doorway as Jack spoke. The man was in a tie and a gray jacket, with a matching bowler on his head. He had an angular frame and a narrow jaw. "I might object to that, Counsellor, on the grounds of a conflict of interest."

The man was Nathan Springer, prosecuting attorney. Jack had never liked him.

All indications were that Montana would be achieving statehood this year or next. If so, the state would be divided up into counties, and a position like prosecuting attorney would likely become an elected office. When that happened, Jack figured Nathan Springer would no longer be a problem because the man had the personality of a coyote. But, at the moment, the position was hired by the Town, and Springer was the one they hired.

"Why, Springer, it didn't take long for the scent of blood to reach you, scavenger that you are."

Springer gave a smile, a smile that had no warmth or humor behind it. "Just doing my job, McCabe. It might behoove you to start doing yours. You can't take this case because it would be an obvious conflict of interest."

"And how does your warped excuse for a mind come to that conclusion?"

"Because if the Judge should win this case, then he will be in your debt. You would love to have a Territorial Judge in your debt, wouldn't you?"

Jack hadn't thought of that. But before he could comment, Judge Mack piped up. "Don't matter none, anyway. Cain't afford Jack, and I won't take charity from any man."

Springer looked at Tom. "I suppose you have questioned the witnesses, Marshal?"

Tom nodded his head. "I've gotten statements from everyone involved."

"Of course, those statements are not valid because the prosecuting attorney wasn't present. Let's start again. Might as well get comfortable, everyone, because we're going to be here for a while."

He looked at Jack. "And your services are not needed, McCabe. And your presence here is unacceptable."

Judge Mack looked at Jack. "It's all right, Jack."

"Mrs. Middleton," Springer said to Aunt Ginny, "You're not needed here, either."

Ginny looked at her nephew. "Come on, Jack. I'm heading out to the ranch for dinner this evening, but I have time to buy you a cup of coffee at the Second Chance."

"Even better, why don't you join Nina and me for a cup of tea? I was just heading home."

"That sounds wonderful." She tossed a glance at Springer. "Something certain people in this town seem not to be."

Springer said to her, "I mean nothing personal, Mrs. Middleton."

"Mister Springer, I have found there is very little personal about you." She fixed him with what she called the Gaze. Jack had seen her administer it more than once throughout the years. He thought Springer did well not to take a step backward and visibly wilt in front of her.

With a grin, Jack held out his arm to his aunt, she took it, and they headed out the door.

10

JOHNNY LOWERED himself into a hot bath, his stiff back and hips telling him he was getting old. To think eighty Red Angus over a three-mile cattle drive could wear him out like this—he winced at the memory of the old cattle drives from years ago, when he and the boys had brought herds of Longhorns to the railheads down in Wyoming and Kansas.

In a way, he hated that those days were gone. Just ten years earlier, this valley had seemed so remote. But he had to admit, in spite of himself, as the heat of the bath worked its way into his aching back and hip muscles, he was glad he and the boys hadn't been attempting to bring those Red Angus beeves all the way south to Cheyenne. For the moment, he found himself glad the railroad was here. Though he would never admit it to Dusty or Charles. He hated to admit it even to himself.

He came downstairs in freshly laundered jeans and a clean white shirt. His boots were the same ones he had worn during the day. He never wore different boots, not even to church, but he wiped off the dust and shined the spurs a little.

He left his gunbelt upstairs, looped over the corner of a bedroom chair. A time had been when he wouldn't have gone twenty feet without a gun on his hip. But he was working toward putting away the jitteriness that had plagued him since his time with the Rangers down in Texas, years ago.

Johnny had worn his hair long ever since he spent a winter with a band of Shoshone here in the valley, almost thirty years earlier. According to Shoshone custom, a warrior cut his hair when in grief, and Johnny had cut his short when Lura was killed. And then he had done so again when Chen had been killed the previous summer. This time, he had decided not to let it grow back. The shorter hair sort of symbolized a new beginning for him, as he stopped allowing himself to obsessively yearn for a way of life that was fast slipping away and he began embracing life today.

Jessica was at work in the kitchen, and Em and Cora were helping.

"When is everyone due?" Johnny said.

Jessica glanced at a clock mounted on the wall. "Any time."

"Think I'll pour a scotch and wait on the porch, out of your way."

With a scotch in one hand, he headed out to the porch. He leaned one hand on the rail and let his gaze wander over the view in front of him. Years ago, when they had first settled this valley, he had a view of nearly half a mile from this porch. The valley floor was mostly flat and grassy, and it provided good grazing.

Today, trees had grown up along the river, blocking some of the view. Smaller groves of trees scattered throughout the valley floor had grown tall, further blocking his view. But he could see smoke rising from the chimney of the Harding farmhouse. And he could still see a couple of peaks standing hazy in the distance.

Soon the guests arrived. Matt and Peddie first, with news that Hiram was in town. Then came Ginny and Sam, telling them about the shooting at the Cattleman's Club. Nate and Sarah arrived—they had no news but instead brought an apple pie fresh out of the oven.

As they ate, the conversation focused mainly on the shooting. What had really happened? Could Judge Mack have shot down a man in cold blood? The only witnesses were the ruffian Gabe Quint and Hiram, and Maybelle. She had said it all happened so fast she wasn't sure what she saw, but Quint and Hiram were claiming it was murder.

Johnny cut into a piece of steak. "What's Hiram doing in town?"

Matt said, "He visited us earlier. He works for a group that apparently wants to buy this ranch."

Johnny shook his head. "We're not selling. Because of that acreage we sold east of the valley, we don't need the money."

After dinner, Johnny returned to the front porch. The sun was now down and a summer evening was upon them. Ginny took a rocker that was on the porch, and she had a glass of wine in one hand. Sam stood with a cigar smoldering away clenched between his thumb and forefinger. Johnny sort of half-leaned, half-sat against the porch railing. He also had a cigar in one hand.

He and Jessica were being prudent with their spending, to make the money from the sale of the land last as long as possible. They had even invested some of it in the stock market, with Jack's guidance. But one indulgence Johnny allowed was a couple of boxes of good cigars.

Matt sat on a small bench against the wall, and he was working on a glass of scotch.

"Tell me, John," Ginny said, "just what do you know about Judge Mack? He's been the circuit judge since the Town of Jubilee was founded, and Jack has gotten to know him to some degree. But the Town Council is meeting tomorrow for an inquest, and I know so little about him."

Matt shook his head. "That's not how things will be done once we have statehood. An inquest is a thing of the judicial system and should be overseen by a judge."

"Statehood will be nice, if and when it happens, but right now we have to get things done using whatever resources are available to us. Governor White will have to appoint a new judge, but he likely won't do that unless charges are filed, and that won't happen without an inquest."

Johnny grinned. "That's why Jack calls this territorial judicial system a glorified kangaroo court."

Ginny nodded her head. "I fully agree. Alisha Summers and I and the others on the Town Council aren't judges. We're businessmen and women. But, for right now, this system is all we have. So," she looked at Johnny, "what can you tell me about Judge Mack?"

"I met him once briefly, years ago in Texas, but I've heard a lot about him."

"He's such an odd character. How did such a man get himself appointed as a territorial judge?"

"He actually has a law degree, from somewhere back East."

Ginny blinked her eyes with surprise. "Are you serious?"

Sam nodded his head in agreement with Johnny. "Yale, I think. I've heard about him over the years."

Johnny said, "He came west as a young man, probably not long after law school. I don't know why. Something must have happened to make him leave his life back east behind."

Matt nodded. "So many men come west to get a fresh start, running from something that happened back east."

"Whatever his reasons were for coming west, be became a gunfighter, a man you didn't want to cross. Sometimes he was on the side of the law and sometimes not. It depended on what he thought was right. I suppose he answered to his own definition of justice."

Ginny grinned. "Sounds like someone else I know."

Sam took a draw from his cigar. "I had the chance to meet him once. He was in a saloon, drinking whiskey and flirting with one of the women who worked there. He has a way of drawing attention to himself and I wanted to do just the opposite, so I stood at the bar and had a drink and got out of there."

"He's seeing a girl in town. A former saloon woman, herself. Angie Thacker. A sweet girl. She works for Alisha Summers, at the Cattleman's."

Johnny nodded. "She waited on Jessica and me

when we had dinner there a couple of years ago."

"She's not much older than Bree. An odd thing, she calls him *Judge*, not by whatever his given name is. I don't think I've ever heard his given name."

Sam said, "He's been called *Judge* forever, I think. Long before he actually became a judge. But his name is Hannibal McIntyre."

Ginny took a sip of wine. "The way it stands now, a man was shot at the Cattleman's, and two witnesses, including Hiram McCabe, claim it was in cold blood. And, if I know Jack, he's going to take the case. As such, I'm going to need to know as much about the gruffy and unseemly Judge Mack as I can."

Johnny took a draw from his cigar. "I'll tell you all I know."

Sam nodded. "I'll fill in the blanks, if I can."

"The first I ever heard of him was in Texas, back when Matt, Joe and I were working on a ranch."

Matt said, "That would be Breaker Grant's spread. It was the late 1850s, and we were on the run and using assumed names."

Johnny looked at Ginny. "I told you all about that, one Christmas night a few years ago."

Ginny nodded.

"We were in the northeastern side of Texas, not far from the Oklahoma line. But in southern Texas is the town called Wardtown."

"Joe worked there as a deputy for a while."

"That's right. The first time I ever heard about Judge Mack was when he was doing what Joe did, working as a deputy marshal in Wardtown."

11

1857

HANNIBAL McINTYRE WAS a young man and pretty much everyone called him Mack. He was young but his face was already leathery from years of riding into the sun and wind. His hair fell to his shoulders and he had a beard that grew like a wild bush. And he wore a Colt Dragoon at his right hip and a matching one at his left.

He had gotten hired as deputy town marshal, and he was in the town marshal's office one night drinking what was left of a cold cup of coffee while the marshal walked his rounds.

Marshal Watkins was an older man, with a long, white mustache, but he struck Mack as capable. A former Ranger who had ridden with Captain Morris in the war that was coming to be called the Texas Revolution, more than twenty years earlier.

Mack heard gunshots, and he ran from the marshal's office to see riders tearing away down the street. It was late and most of the windows of the main street were dark, but the saloon was still open and a man stepped out to see what the commotion was all about.

In the light from the saloon door, Mack found Marshal Watkins lying on his back in the street. Blood soaked the front of the marshal's shirt.

"They were robbing the bank," Watkins said, his voice not much more than a whisper. Mack figured a bullet had found a lung. "I surprised 'em. Got one of 'em."

Mack saw one man lying on the boardwalk.

Mack called out for someone to get Doc Mullins, and within a few minutes the doctor came running. He was in a nightshirt and robe, and he clutched a medical bag in one hand. But it was too late. The marshal was gone.

The bartender from the saloon had come out. A man with a bald head and with an apron tied over a round stomach. He knelt over the man the marshal had shot and pressed with his fingers at the man's neck, checking for a pulse. "This one's dead, too."

Then he said, "Hey, I know him. Fred Jenkins. He and his brothers were in my saloon last Saturday. Said they were looking to claim some land and start raising a small herd."

Mack shook his head. "Apparently they were looking more at our bank than they were at starting up a herd."

The doctor said, "I need some men to haul both bodies down to my office, and I'll write up death certificates."

A small crowd had gathered. Mack gave them a long look, going from one man to another. "I had a father once, but Marshal Watkins was more of a father to me than my real father ever was. You men, every one of you, can now consider yourselves deputized. Every one of you that can ride."

One of them said, "Pardon me, Deputy, but do you have the authority to deputize men?"

Mack slapped the gun at his side. "This here gives me the authority. Come mornin', we're goin' after the rest of the Jenkins brothers. We ride at first light."

They caught the Jenkins brothers the following afternoon. There were four brothers and, when the brothers saw the posse bearing down on them, they rode for an outcropping of rocks, pulled their rifles from their saddles and took cover.

Mack and the men with him took cover behind some trees. The brothers fired, and Mack and the posse shot back. Bullets tore into the wood of the trees and zinged from the rocks the Jenkins brothers hid behind.

Then the Jenkins boys stopped firing.

The bartender was behind an old oak. "What's happening?"

"Don't know, Mort." Mack was behind a double-trunked birch. "Maybe they ran out of ammunition."

"We surrender!" one of them called out.

Mort looked at Mack. Despite his size, Mort could ride and knew how to use a gun. "Think they're faking?"

"Let's find out." Mack stepped out from behind the tree where he had taken cover. With his revolver in hand, he started walking toward the rocks.

Three of the Jenkins boys stood up, their hands in the air.

Mack said, "Where's the fourth one?"

"He's dead."

Mack approached until he was within thirty feet of them. Mort was behind him.

The Jenkins brothers looked more like saddle bums than hardened outlaws. They were staring at Mack with fear in their eyes. Like they had said, the fourth brother was on the ground, dead.

The oldest one of them, who was maybe thirty, said, "We turn ourselves in."

Mack said to Mort. "Toss him your gun."

Mort looked at him. "Give him a gun?"

"I want him to have a loaded gun in his hand when he dies. I ain't no murderer."

Mort tossed his revolver to Jenkins, who caught it. "You can't do this. You gotta take us in so we can face a judge. You're a lawman."

"You got that right." Mack cocked his gun and aimed it at him. "I'm a lawman. And I'm also your judge and jury."

He pulled the trigger.

When they got back to town, Mort told the story to anyone who would listen. And from then on, the deputy was called Judge Mack.

12

GINNY DIDN'T KNOW whether to laugh or be appalled. "Are you serious? That's how he got his name?"

Johnny nodded. Sam said, "That's the story I heard, too."

Johnny took another draw of his cigar. "Not much has been said of him, before he rode into Wardtown and started working for Mose Watkins. In fact, more is said of Watkins than of Mack."

Matt nodded his head. "During our time in Texas, Mose Watkins was talked about a lot. His time with the Rangers, and the years later. He's almost a legend."

Ginny shook her head. "How barbaric. To think a man like Mack got himself somehow appointed to a judgeship is unthinkable."

"It might sound barbaric by today's standards, but it was a different time. Such things were more common. Justice was often decided by a man's conscience, and with a gun."

Johnny nodded his head. "Even today, it's sometimes done that way."

Ginny looked at him. "Mister Chen, last year."

"What I did was probably against the law. But if I hadn't, they would have gone free. The worst that would have happened is them being deported back to China, where they would have been praised for killing Chen."

Sam nodded his head. "What you did was justice. Plain and simple."

Ginny looked at him and then back to Johnny. "I suppose we don't know what the marshal meant to him. Maybe Mack felt justified in the shooting."

Johnny nodded his head. "Often, learning the truth can shed a new light on things."

"I wonder if that was what he was doing this afternoon, when he shot that man. Administering justice."

"I suppose we won't know, until after we hear

both sides at tomorrow's inquest."

"*We?*"

"You bet. I wouldn't miss it for the world."

Hiram stood in his hotel room. He glanced over to the chest of drawers, and the empty spot where his whiskey bottle had once stood. He thought a belt or two would do him good, considering the day he had, but he no longer had that option.

He said to the man behind him, "I don't feel right about what you're asking me to do."

Quint leaned against the door jamb-the door hung open and the empty hallway was behind him, and he gripped Hiram's whiskey bottle in one hand. "I don't care what you think feels right or not. And you can bet Mister Randall don't, either. You're on the payroll. You do what Mister Randall wants. Simple as that. He wants Judge Mack out of the picture so we can have Governor White appoint a new judge. One that'll be more favorable to Mister Randall's interests."

Hiram looked at Quint. "We were both there. We saw fully well what happened. That man drew his gun and shot first. Well, they both shot at nearly the same time, but the Judge would have been killed if he hadn't shot the man down."

"At that inquest tomorrow, you're gonna tell' em what I told you to tell 'em. Getting Mack out of the way like this will be a lot easier than trying to put a bullet in him. The man's getting old but, back in his day, men what tried to kill him tended to turn up dead. Mack's old now, but it's still a risk going up ag'in him. Johnny McCabe is old, too, but they say he beat a man to death last year. A Chinese man who was built like a bull. So you say what I tell you to say, and it'll make our lives a lot easier."

"I can see how it'll make your life easier. But how will it benefit me?"

"You don't want me to report to Mister Randall that you're turning on him. When men disappoint

Mister Randall, they also have a way of turning up dead."

Quint turned away. "And wear a suit and tie tomorrow, will you? You look like a clown in them range clothes. Anyone taking one look at you can tell you ain't done a lick of real work in your life."

Hiram felt his ire rising. No one talked to him that way. "Quint, I want my whiskey bottle back and I want it back now."

Quint looked over his shoulder at him with a look of amusement and surprise. "Oh, you do, do you?"

"That's right."

Quint turned and charged at him. Hiram barely had time to gasp before Quint grabbed him by the shirt, ripping buttons free as he did so, and threw Hiram onto the bed. Hiram bounced away from the mattress and landed on the floor, and before he could blink his eyes or catch his breath, Quint straddled him and held a knife to his throat. Where the knife had come from, Hiram didn't know. He hadn't seen one on Quint's person.

Quint spoke through clenched teeth. "I'd just as soon cut your throat right here and now and watch you bleed out all over the floor. Or maybe cut off an ear and watch you scream like a little girl. But Mister Randall is gonna need you to testify tomorrow. Comprende?"

Hiram nodded. He did so carefully because the blade felt sharp against his neck.

Quint rose to his feet and began walking back toward the doorway. "Get some sleep. I want you sharp in court tomorrow. You speak that sissy courtroom talk better'n I do. You'll make the better witness. You do good tomorrow, and you'll make Mister Randall happy. You don't do good, and I'll stick a knife in you."

And Quint stepped out into the hallway and was gone.

Hiram sat up and brought one finger to a raw spot on his throat. He brought his finger away and saw a tiny smear of blood. That man's knife had cut him.

Hiram shook his head and said, to no one because he was now alone, "How did I ever fall in with these people?"

He still felt stunned over what Quint had said about Aloysius Randall earlier in the day. If it was all true, then Randall was no one Hiram wanted to be working with. Hiram intended to head back to California as soon as possible, whereupon he would sell his stock in the ventures he shared with Randall. But first, he had to live through tomorrow. And to do that, he was going to have to do something he had never done before. Perjure himself.

He got to his feet and glanced at the clock mounted on one wall. Twelve past nine. The bar downstairs would still be open.

He headed out the door that was hanging open and went downstairs to the hotel lounge. He came back with another bottle of whiskey.

He shut the door and sat at the edge of the bed, and he pulled the cork free from the bottle. He didn't even bother to fetch one of the glasses that were on the chest of drawers where the first whiskey bottle had stood. He tipped the bottle and let the whiskey burn its way down.

Jack McCabe let his head sink into the pillow. Nina was beside him, long since asleep. The room was mostly dark. The only light came from a lamp on a small table by his side of the bed, and the lamp was turned so low the flame barely survived.

Jack shut his eyes and waited for sleep to take him. But it didn't. He thought peaceful thoughts. Riding a horse through the mountains, or having a picnic lunch with Nina in the valley. Didn't work. He opened his eyes.

He sat up in bed and thought about going downstairs. Maybe a shot of bourbon as a toddy would help him sleep.

Nina said, "Can't you sleep?"

Apparently she wasn't as asleep as Jack had thought. "No. I guess not."

She rolled over to look at him. She was no more than a formless outline in the near darkness of the room, and he couldn't imagine he looked much different to her.

She said, "You're thinking about that inquest tomorrow, aren't you?"

"Judge Mack needs me."

"There's another attorney in town."

Jack knew who she was talking about. "Origen Scott. Fresh in from Philadelphia. I've had coffee with him. He's a good enough sort, but he has no experience at anything more than drawing up a will or a deed."

"Judge Mack said he can't afford you, and he won't accept you pro bono because it feels like charity to him."

Jack shook his head. "Doesn't matter. He needs me."

"Has anyone ever told you that you approach law like a gunhawk?"

He grinned. "Yeah. You have, a time or two."

"Or maybe, more appropriately, a knight in buckskin. That's what Aunt Ginny calls you McCabe men."

Jack nodded. "She's said that a time or two, also."

"Why do you suppose you're all like that?"

Jack shrugged. "Something we learned from Pa. He says he learned it from his father. Family tradition, I suppose."

Jack heard something downstairs. A tapping sound. "You hear that?"

"I think someone's at the front door."

"At this hour? It has to be near eleven o'clock."

He shouldered into a robe, pulling it tight over his nightshirt. "You wait here."

"Who could it be?"

"It's probably nothing."

And yet, he went to a bureau and slid open a

drawer, and he pulled out a revolver. After all, he was his father's son.

He went downstairs and turned up a lamp in the parlor. He checked the loads in the pistol, and then he headed for the door. Whoever was out there was still rapping. It sounded loud, now that he was downstairs.

He opened the door and saw a woman standing on the front step. It took him a moment to realize who it was. "Angie Thacker?"

She nodded her head. "It's so late. I hate to bother you."

"Are you alone?"

She nodded her head.

He said, "What're you doing, walking the streets alone at this hour?"

Jack heard footsteps behind him, and Nina's voice. "Let her in, Jack. I'll go put on some water for tea."

Angie looked tired. She was in the same blouse and skirt Jack had seen her in earlier, and the same kerchief was tied over her hair.

Jack offered her a chair at the kitchen table while he got a fire going in the stove and then Nina filled a kettle of water for boiling.

Angie said, "That man the Judge shot—he was in my room, trying to attack me. Thought I was in the old business I used to be in, and he wanted a tumble and wouldn't take no for an answer and he started getting rough. The Judge stopped him. The Judge beat him up right there in the room and then dragged him out and threw him down the stairs."

"Nothing I wouldn't have done," Jack said.

Nina sat at the table, across from Angie, while the water was heating. "Do you think the Judge actually just shot the man down?"

Angie shook her head. "He says he didn't, that he shot because the man was gonna shoot him, and I believe him. But he was so mad at that man. I'll admit, I wanted the Judge to break his neck."

Jack sat beside Nina. "You can't say that tomorrow at the inquest."

"But it's the truth."

He nodded his head. "But there are ways to present the truth that can look bad."

"I don't understand."

Jack drew a breath. "Let's say Nina makes us some biscuits and you have one, and you don't like it."

Nina looked at him. "Hey."

He grinned. "Just a hypothetical."

She gave him a reluctant nod of her head.

Jack looked at Angie. "So, when Nina asks how the biscuit is, what do you say?"

Angie crinkled up her nose as she gave it a little thought. "I guess I would give a polite lie and say it was good. Nina's a friend and I wouldn't want to hurt her feelings."

"But what if you were under oath?"

Nina looked at him. "Will she be under oath tomorrow? If she's called to testify?"

Jack gave a noncommittal shrug of his shoulders. "Sort of."

"Would she be under penalty of perjury?"

He gave the shrug again. "It's never really been tested. No precedent has been set in this sort of frontier makeshift court. And there probably won't be because it looks like we might have statehood within a year or less, the way things are going. Then there won't be any more things like an inquest held by a town council. We'll have county and state court systems."

Angie said, "What's all that mean?"

"It means tomorrow is not really court. It'll be a glorified meeting of the Town Council to determine whether or not the Judge will be charged. He'll testify, and you might be called to testify, too. You will both have to give an oath to tell the truth, like in court. But it's not really court."

She nodded her head. "I think I understand."

"So, in our hypothetical situation, Nina has baked

a biscuit that you don't much like."

"What's that mean? Hypo..."

"*Hypothetical.* It means a situation that isn't real, but we're presenting it is as a sort of mental exercise."

"Kind of like a *what if.*"

"Exactly. In our hypothetical situation, Nina made a biscuit you don't like. You don't want to hurt her feelings, but you don't want to lie, so you tell her you liked it. But if you were under oath, you couldn't lie because if you got caught it would be a crime. A felony. So you tell the truth but you do it in a careful way. Instead of saying you don't like it, you could say, *It's not bad. Not bad at all.* Not a lie, and it wouldn't hurt her feelings."

"But it *is* a lie. Telling her the bad biscuit ain't bad is a lie."

"No, it's not, not really, because the term *bad* is subjective." He didn't wait to see if she knew the term. "That means it's a matter of opinion. What one person calls bad might be different than what another calls it. So you're not lying. You're just being purposely vague, but without saying that you're being vague."

She frowned a little. "Sounds a little like lawyerin' is about telling a lie but hiding it as the truth."

Nina laughed. "I think you hit the nail right on the head."

Jack said, "Maybe, but sometimes it has to be done, if it's for a good cause. The Judge is a good man. It would be wrong to send him to prison or the gallows."

Angie nodded.

"For some reason, those men are saying they saw him do something he didn't do. A good lawyer has to find out why and take their story apart, and to protect his client from having his own story taken apart by the other attorney. An effective lawyer can make a truthful person sound like they're saying something they're not. That's what I don't want Nathan Springer doing to you."

"Do you think he would?"

Jack shrugged. "I've know the man a few years.

He strikes me as one who is more interested in building a career than he is in seeking justice."

Nina checked the water. The kettle was hissing a little, meaning it might be time to pour the water and add some tea. "So, if Angie is asked if she thinks the Judge is capable of shooting a man down, what should she say?"

"She shouldn't answer the question. An objection should be filed under the grounds of irrelevance. Asking a person's opinion is in no way a presentation of evidence."

Angie looked at him. "So, I have to say that objection thing?"

Jack shook his head. "The Judge's attorney is the one who will do the talking. He'll say something like, *Objection. Irrelevant.*"

"The Judge has hired Orrie Scott as his lawyer. Do you think Orrie is smart enough to know to say that objection thing? I mean, he's a nice enough feller and all, but does he know enough about the lawyerin' business to know what to say?"

Jack shrugged. "I hope so."

She shook her head. "I want you to be the Judge's lawyer. He said no because he can't afford you. Orrie don't charge as much. I said, what if Jack don't charge as much? What if he lowers his rates? The Judge said he won't take charity. Same thing he said earlier."

"I can't make him take me on if he doesn't want to."

"But can you be there?"

"Town Council meetings are open to the public, so I can be in the audience, but I won't be able to take part in it."

Nina brought over a cup of tea for Angie and one for herself. Jack wasn't a tea drinker. "What if you're there to represent Angie? To be *her* attorney?"

Jack's brows went up. "Now, there's an idea."

Angie said, "But I ain't got no money."

"I'll take you on pro bono."

"What's that mean? That bone thing?"

"It means I'll represent you for free. That's what I offered the Judge and he told me he wouldn't take charity."

She gave a long, "Ohhh."

Now she got it. "But he has a point. I don't like taking charity neither."

"It's not charity. You're a friend. You've given me a free cup of coffee at the Cattlemans' before, right?"

She nodded.

"That wasn't charity and neither is this. It's just one friend helping out another."

"Then will you do it? Will you be there tomorrow to be my lawyer?"

He nodded. "Absolutely."

Nina gave Jack a smile. "My knight in buckskin."

13

COME MORNING, Hiram stopped in front of Quint's door and rapped his knuckles against it. No answer. He thought of trying the door to see if it was locked, but his survival instinct kicked in instead. If Quint was in there, he might not take too kindly to someone walking into his room uninvited. Hiram wasn't so much concerned about Quint's feelings. He just didn't want to get shot. So he knocked again on the door.

"What you want?" It was Quint's whiskey-soaked voice, but it came from down the hall.

Hiram saw Quint at the top of the stairs. Saddlebags were draped over one shoulder and he had a Winchester in one hand. "I'm heading down to breakfast. I didn't want you to come to my room and find me not there. I wouldn't want you to come looking for me and stick a knife in me, at least until I've had my morning coffee."

"Why would I care where you are?"

"Today's the day of the inquest. It starts in two hours. Where have you been?"

"Not that it's any business of yours, but I've been what they call surveillin' the enemy."

"What does that mean?"

Quint pushed past him and then opened his door. It had been unlocked. "It means if you want to know what they're up to, you gotta keep an eye on 'em."

He stepped into his room and Hiram followed.

Hiram said, "Just what does that mean? What enemy?"

"The McCabes, you idjit." He dropped the saddlebags on the bed, and then set the rifle down beside them.

Hiram looked at him with disbelief. "You've been spying on the ranch?"

Quint nodded with a smile.

Hiram said, "That could get you killed."

"Only if they see me. Been causin' a little trouble, too." He stepped over to a chest of drawers and a small device resting on the top of it. He lifted it up and Hiram could see it was a pair of wire cutters. "Used these on some fence yesterday afternoon. Bought 'em at the general store before I rode out."

"Which general store?"

"Franklin's, down the street from here."

Hiram let out a long sigh and shook his head. "You bought those from Johnny McCabe's daughter. Do you know that?"

Quint frowned at him like he thought he was an idiot. "No I didn't. The sign out front says *Franklin's.*"

"It might say that, but Johnny McCabe's daughter and son-in-law own it. I don't know why it says *Franklin's.* That's not their name."

"Some young jasper behind the counter sold 'em to me. There was a girl there, too. A smart-mouthed kid."

Hiram nodded. "How long will it be before they connect one thing to another and figure it was you?"

Quint set the wire cutters back down. "I didn't give 'em my name."

"You didn't have to. You might not realize it, but you have a way of making an impression."

Johnny stepped out behind the house, with a rope coiled up in one hand. He was in a range shirt with a vest on over it, and his Stetson was pulled down over his temples. His gun was at his hip and he held a rope coiled up in one hand. His plan was to drop a loop over a horse and saddle him up for a ride into town. The inquest started in a couple of hours, but he hoped to get there early so he could have a cup of coffee first.

Charles came riding up. Tall and thin, and he had taken to wearing a ten gallon hat which made him look even taller. "Mornin', Pa. Want me to saddle up a horse for you?"

Johnny shook his head. "Thanks, but I'll do it."

"We've got to hire us a wrangler."

Johnny nodded in agreement. "As soon as I find the right man. You know how I feel about wranglers."

Charles swung out of the saddle. "He's the most important man on the ranch because he takes care of our horses."

"And a man needs a good horse beneath him."

"I fully agree." Charles began leading his horse toward the house. "Is the coffee hot?"

"Was when I was in there."

"I'll grab me a cup and then I'm meeting Dusty out at the east section of the pasture. He was riding past that last night and saw the barbed wire had been cut, but he couldn't fix it. It was getting late and the light wasn't good."

Johnny stopped walking and looked at him. "Cut?"

Charles nodded his head.

"I was planning on attending the inquest today but maybe I should ride out there with you."

Charles shook his head. "Dusty and I can take care of it. Bree's riding into town for the inquest too, and I know she would like to see you. She hasn't had a visit with you in a week or so."

Johnny nodded his head. "Every time she's been here at the house I've been off working."

"I'm gonna go grab some coffee." Charles continued his way toward the house.

Johnny returned his attention to the remuda that was grazing out back. Thunder wasn't in sight. Probably off running in the mountains again. Ash stood about three hundred feet away with his nose down in the grass. A couple of mares were frolicking about and some geldings were off by the edge of the woods.

The underbrush was so tangled at the edge of the woods that a horse couldn't get through if it tried, which is why this section of grassy acreage out behind the house made the perfect natural remuda.

Once in a while a horse ran out past the front of

the house but it wouldn't run far. It was happening more often though, and Johnny was weighing the idea of fencing off part of the acreage out back against the manpower involved.

Dozens of fence posts would have to be cut and brought down from one of the ridges surrounding the valley, and then more for fence rail, unless they went with barbed wire but Johnny didn't like that idea. He didn't want any of the horses getting cut up on the danged stuff.

Johnny had a couple of geldings in mind for the ride into town. But as he walked out toward where one of them grazed, a gelding that was a sorrel with a splash of white between his eyes, Ash lifted his head and came trotting over.

Ash had made it known more than once that when Johnny was going somewhere, Ash wanted to be the one to take him there, and he was making it known again right now. But Johnny knew the inquest could take a couple of hours and he didn't want to leave a high spirited, half broke horse like Ash at the hitching rail for two long hours.

Johnny stroked Ash's nose with one hand and said, "Not this time. Next time, I promise."

Johnny rode into town on the sorrel gelding. Bree had named the horse *Unicorn*, because of the stripe of white between his eyes, in her on-going way of giving horses names that she found amusing. She had been doing that since she was a little girl.

A mare she called *Flame* stood at the hitching rail in front of the Second Chance. Charles had said Bree would be here, and Flame was usually her horse of choice. Johnny noticed she didn't give her own horses funny names.

He stepped into the saloon side of the Second Chance to find Hunter sliding tables around, preparing for the inquest. Since there was no town hall, such events were usually hosted by Hunter and Aunt Ginny here in the barroom.

Hunter had slid back a number of tables, but he had brought three together at the front of the room.

Aunt Ginny stood with her arms folded, looking through her spectacles at Hunter's work. "Good. Those three tables should suffice for the Town Council. We'll also need a table for Judge Mack and his attorney, and one for Mister Springer."

She glanced over her shoulder toward the doorway. "Good morning, John."

He nodded to her. "I see you're hard at work telling people what to do."

"Some things never change," Hunter said with a grin.

"Is the coffee still hot?"

Ginny said, "If you can call that mud you drink coffee."

But she said it with a little grin. Part of their on-going trading of barbs.

"Sounds like it's just the way I like it."

Hunter filled a cup and handed it to Johnny.

Bree was at one table and Johnny joined her. She was in a jacket and an ankle-length skirt, and Johnny noticed her gunbelt was buckled about her hips. She seldom rode far from home without it.

She mentioned the barbed wire. "Dusty rode by our cabin on the way home last night and told us he thought it had been cut."

Johnny nodded. "Yeah. I saw Charles before I rode on in. He mentioned it."

"Who would cut barbed wire?"

"Someone wanting to get himself shot?"

She grinned and took a sip of coffee. "I can't imagine who would do it. I doubt an Angus can roam too far. Dusty and Charles will just have to round up any strays. It shouldn't take 'em too long."

Johnny took a drink of his coffee. "I saw you rode Flame in this morning. She doing well?"

Bree nodded. "You have Ash?"

He shook his head. "I rode in on that horse you named Unicorn."

"You didn't ride Mopsy?"

Another gelding, with an extra long mane. She had said the horse had hair like a mop.

He shook his head with a grin. "I'll admit, I have a little problem riding a horse named Mopsy."

That got a chuckle out of her. "I'm thinking maybe we should try to breed Flame and Ash. That would make one heck of a colt."

Then something occurred to Johnny. He thought about the conversation he had with Charles about hiring a wrangler and how he was looking for the right man. Maybe the right man was a woman.

"Bree, how would you like a job?"

She looked at him. "What kind of job?"

"Wrangler, for the ranch. I know you already own a part of the place, but now you would get a steady salary, too."

"Is that Charles' idea?"

Johnny shook his head. "Mine. Just occurred to me. You would be perfect for the job. Except..."

"Except what?"

He shrugged his shoulders. "Well, it would mean hefting them heavy saddles up onto a horse's back. That's a lot of work for a lady."

She gave him an indignant look, but she knew he was kidding her so there was a grin included. "Hey. I'm no lady. I'm your daughter."

"You're actually both, you just don't know it. So how about it? You want the job?"

"I suppose I should talk it over with Charles. We make all major decisions together."

"What do you think he'll say?"

"Well," she smiled, "I 'spect he'll say yes."

Jack walked in and came over to the table. "Here to watch the proceedings?"

Johnny nodded. "Thought I'd start the day with some light entertainment."

"I'll get a cup of coffee and join you, if you don't mind."

Once he had his coffee and had pulled out a chair, Johnny said, "So, you a spectator or working?"

"Angie Thacker hired me to represent her, should she be called to the stand."

Nathan Springer walked up to the table. He had walked in behind Jack, and as he approached the table he heard what Jack said.

"That's a conflict of interest, McCabe. We already talked about that sort of thing."

"First of all, I would have thought you'd learned by now, I have little interest in your opinions. Second of all, I'm not representing the Judge, I'm representing Miss Thacker. If you call her to the stand and try to bully her, I'll be in her corner."

Springer gave a scoffing chuckle. "Is that supposed to intimidate me?"

Bree rolled her eyes. "Will you go away, Springer? We were having a pleasant time until you slithered up."

Johnny grinned and Jack almost choked on his coffee.

Springer looked at her like a stern school master trying to stare down a student. "A woman should keep out of matters that don't concern her."

She sat back and folded her arms. "Have you ever faced a grizzly?"

"What does that have to do with anything?"

"How long do you think you could last against a full grown grizzly?"

Jack stopped laughing long enough to say, "Probably about five seconds."

"I faced a grizzly that was charging at me, and I kept a steady hand and put a bullet between his eyes. And I was only ten."

Johnny said, "It happened. No exaggeration."

Springer shook his head. "Again I say, what does that have to do with anything?"

Jack said, "It means she could chew you up and

spit you out."

Johnny leveled his gaze at Springer. "Treat her with respect. That's not a request."

Springer stood his ground, for two seconds, like he was considering an attempt to stare down Johnny McCabe. But he thought better of it and turned away.

"What do you suppose is wrong with him?" Jack asked.

Bree reached for her coffee. "His bloomers are too tight."

Jack laughed again.

Johnny took a sip of coffee. "I hired us a wrangler, today."

"Oh yeah? Who?"

"Let's just say I think the remuda will be safe from grizzlies."

14

THEY SAT and drank coffee while people from the town drifted in. One was a man about sixty with a stoic look and a long white beard. He was in a tie and jacket, and he now owned the Randall House hotel.

"Squire Mortensen," Johnny said. "Chair of the Town Council."

Jack nodded his head. "Too bad he didn't have a law degree. Then you know what they could call him? Squire Mortensen, Esquire."

Bree shook her head with a grin. "You clearly don't have enough to keep your mind busy."

In came Aaron Digby. About Johnny's age, not quite so tall but with a round stomach. His hair was receding and he had bushy mutton chops. His wife was with him. He got her seated at a table behind Johnny then took his place at the table reserved for the Town Council. He was the manager of the local bank.

Alisha Summers stepped in with Maybelle— Johnny realized he had never heard Maybelle's last name. She had been introduced to him a few years ago as Miss Maybelle and nothing else. Both were wearing little hats pinned to their hair and had shawls wrapped about their shoulders.

Johnny and Jack got to their feet, and the women came to say hello.

Johnny said, "You are more than welcome to sit with us if you would like."

"That would be nice," Miss Maybelle said. "Thank you."

"I will have to join them at the front table soon," Alisha said. "But I'll sit with you all a while. You're much better company than the stodgy old men who make up most of the Town Council."

Once the ladies were seated, Johnny waved Hunter over and Miss Maybelle and Miss Alisha ordered tea.

Jack said to Alisha, "Where's Angie?"

"She's at the jail with the Judge."

Johnny shook his head. "The jail is no place for her."

"Couldn't talk her out of it. But that's where I would be if I was in her place."

Hunter brought over two cups of tea. "We do a lot of business on days like this. Too bad Dusty ain't here to lend a hand. He and Mister Chen were the best help I ever had here."

Johnny nodded. "Dusty's busy at the ranch. Got some fence wire that broke. Dusty thinks it might have been cut."

That got Hunter's attention. "Do tell. Any idea who it might have been?"

Johnny shook his head. "None at all."

"I'd appreciate it if you'd let me know if you find out anything. I helped build that place with you. It'll always be close to my heart."

Ginny set note pads at the tables for the Council members.

Alisha said, "If you'll excuse me, I'd like to talk with Miss Ginny for a few minutes before the proceedings begin."

They watched Alisha hurry over to speak with Ginny. Bree said, "The only two women on the Town Council."

Jack nodded his head. "I wonder if that'll change once we gain statehood. You don't usually see women allowed into politics."

"I can't imagine why anyone would want to be involved in it. Seems like one headache after another."

Folks continued filing into the room. Wasn't long before all of the tables were taken and men began sitting along the bar like it was a long bench. Sam Middleton brought in chairs from the restaurant half of the establishment but soon there was an overflow crowd and people were standing against the back wall.

Nina and Myrna came in. Jack said to Nina, "I

thought you decided to stay home."

"I did, but the more I thought about it, the more I figured I can't miss this. I went to the office and talked Myrna into joining me."

Myrna said, "I was planning to stay and sort the mail, but it hasn't arrived yet. Now I know why."

She glanced at the crowd standing at the back of the room. "There's Edwin Merkle, our illustrious postmaster, standing at the back wall. He must have given himself the morning off."

Johnny pulled a pocket watch from inside his vest. Almost nine o'clock. As he slid the watch back into its pocket, Tom came in with Judge Mack. The Judge looked like he had just ridden in from the trail, which was normal for him. What struck Johnny as not so normal was seeing him with wrists cuffed.

Origen Scott was with them, and so was Angie. Tom removed the Judge's handcuffs, and Angie gave him a peck on the cheek and then scurried over to Johnny's table to take the chair Miss Alisha had vacated.

"I'm so scared," she said.

Miss Maybelle laid a hand on hers. "Be strong. We're all here for you."

Hiram McCabe and Quint came in. Hiram was once again in the jacket and tie he had been wearing when he arrived in town. He glanced over to the McCabe table but then looked away. *Afraid?* Johnny wondered. *Embarrassed?*

They took chairs at Nathan Springer's table.

Squire Mortensen raised a gavel. "Let's call these proceedings to order."

But he didn't bring the gavel down. "Dang it all. I just realized we don't have anyone here to record the minutes."

He looked over to the McCabe table. "Jack, would you be so kind as to assist?"

Jack stood up. "I would be glad to, Squire, but I'm actually here in an official capacity. I'm attorney for

Miss Thacker, should she be called to the stand."

Myrna got to her feet. "I'll be glad to do it."

Mortensen said, "Why, thank you, Miss Warren."

Springer stood up. "I have to question this. Miss Warren is secretary for Jackson McCabe, and I'm concerned about a potential conflict of interest—"

She cut him off. "Will you shut up for once?"

The barroom exploded with laugher.

Springer looked at Mortensen. "I object."

Mortensen shook his head. "Can't object. We ain't got started yet. I ain't even brought my little hammer down yet."

More laughter. Springer sat down.

There were no chairs left in the building but Hunter found a wooden stool for Myrna to use, and she sat at the side of one of the Town Council tables. Aunt Ginny got her a tablet of paper and a pencil.

"Now then," Mortensen tapped his gavel on the table. "Let's get this shindig rolling."

He looked at Springer. "All right, Counsellor, if you would care to object to somethin', go ahead and start objectin'."

Springer shook his head with resignation. "Forget it."

The crowd laughed again.

Mortensen tapped his gavel to silence the court. "You know, we really should get me something to hit this hammer on, like a judge has."

Judge Mack said, "I don't even use one. I just use an empty beer mug."

Springer couldn't keep silent. "Why on Earth would you want to use an empty beer mug?"

"'Cause you can't use a full one. You'd spill beer everywhere."

The crowd roared as though they were at a theater, watching a show.

Jack looked at his father. "You see why I call this a kangaroo court?"

Johnny nodded his head. "Is this what court is

usually like here?"

"Not much different."

"Old-style frontier justice was so much easier."

Miss Maybelle said, "With all due respect, Mister McCabe, you can't always fight injustice with a gun."

"Really?"

Jack grinned.

Mortensen said, "All right. This here town meeting is called because we have to determine if charges are to be filed against the accused. The accused being Hannibal McIntyre, better known as Judge Mack."

He looked at Myrna. "You getting all this, young lady?"

Her pencil was scurrying across the paper. "Yes, sir. Including the part about the beer mug."

Chuckles and laughter.

Mortensen looked at Judge Mack. "For the record, please state your name."

Mack sat with one leg crossed over the other knee and his arms folded. "Everyone here knows my name. Judge Mack."

Mortensen grinned. "Now, we know for a fact that your mother didn't call you Judge."

"No, but she should have."

Jack joined in the laughter, despite himself.

He saw Origen Scott lean over and say something to the Judge. Probably cautioning him against appearing belligerent. That was what Jack would have told him.

Mortensen said, "Let's record it for the record that the defendant's name is Hannibal McIntyre."

He looked at Springer. "All right, Nathan. You've got the floor. Say your piece."

Springer rose to his feet. He had unbuttoned his jacket as a gentleman was wont to do when he sat. Now he fastened one button and stood between his table and the Town Council.

"We have before us Judge Mack, Hannibal McIntyre, to determine if charges of murder should be brought against him." He spoke in a theatrical tone, his voice bouncing off the back wall of the barroom. "I intend to prove that the Judge willingly and maliciously took his gun in his hand," Springer made a fist and extended his index finger like the barrel of a revolver and aimed it at an imaginary target, "and shot down Harold Higgins in cold blood."

"Harold Higgins?" Judge Mack said. "Was that his name?"

"You didn't even know the name of the man whose life you extinguished?"

"Didn't need to know it. I caught him trying to force himself on Angie and I showed him the error of his ways."

Origen Scott leaned over and spoke to the Judge again.

Springer continued, in a lofty voice, describing the Judge throwing the aforementioned Harold Higgins down the stairs at the Cattleman's Club, then descending the stairs and drawing his gun and putting a bullet in his victim.

The Judge growled the words. "That ain't the way it happened."

Mortensen said, "All right, Nathan. If you're done, let's give Orrie the chance to talk before anyone starts calling any witnesses."

Springer sat down and Origen got to his feet. He cleared his throat twice and forgot to button his jacket.

"Members of the Town Council, I intend to make the case that the shooting was done in self-defense." His voice wavered a little as he spoke.

Jack leaned over to Johnny. "He's in way over his head."

Orrie continued, "Murder charges are not appropriate in this case because the Judge drew his gun only after the deceased drew his."

He stood silently. Then Mortensen said, "Is that it? Are you done?"

Orrie shrugged his shoulders. "I suppose so."

He sat back down.

Springer didn't wait to be invited. He stood and began walking to his spot in front of the tables used by the Town Council. "I would like to call my first witness, Mister Hiram McCabe."

Hiram stepped forth and took a chair reserved for the witnesses. Hunter approached him with a Bible in one hand.

"Place your hand on the Bible."

Hiram did.

"Do you promise to tell the truth, the whole truth, and nothing but the truth, so help you God?"

Hiram nodded his head. "I do."

Johnny leaned over to Jack. "I doubt a regular court would allow the barkeep to be the bailiff."

Jack chuckled. "No. He'll be out of a job once we have statehood and a real county court. Kind of a shame, though. He takes it quite seriously."

Springer said, "Mister McCabe, on the date of June thirteen, did you see the defendant take a gun in his hand and shoot down his victim, the aforementioned Harold Higgins?"

Hiram nodded his head. "I did."

Jack muttered, loud enough for Johnny to hear, "Objection, Orrie. Leading the witness."

But Orrie said nothing.

Springer continued. "Had Mister Higgins drawn his gun when the shot was fired?"

Hiram nodded his head. "Yes, I believe he had."

"But the Judge drew first. Is that correct?"

"It is."

Jack said, "Say something, Orrie."

Springer was still speaking to Hiram, but he turned to face the Town Council. "So, Mister McCabe, is it your opinion that the Judge shot down the deceased in cold blood?"

"It is."

Jack rolled his eyes and shook his head.

Springer said, "I have no further questions."

Springer turned and walked back to his seat.

Mortensen looked at the defense attorney. "All right, Orrie. Have at him."

Orrie stood up. "I really don't have any questions for him, your honor."

"I'm not anyone's honor, Orrie. Just the chair of the Town Council."

Jack rolled his eyes and shook his head, not because Orrie didn't know how to address Mortensen. "He's gotta ask questions. Tear that story apart."

"Do you really see holes in his story?"

Jack looked at his father. "Not specifically. But a lot happened in a very short time. If Orrie could make Hiram seem at least a little less sure of what he thinks he saw, then it would be more difficult for Springer to prove guilt beyond a shadow of a doubt."

Angie said, "I sure wish the Judge would let you be his lawyer."

As they spoke, Hiram headed back to the prosecutor's table.

Springer announced theatrically, "I would now like to call a Mister Gabriel T. Quint to the stand."

Quint walked up to the chair and Hunter swore him in.

"Just who is this jasper?" Johnny asked.

"I think I remember him from a couple of years ago." Jack rubbed his chin as he thought about it. "Yes. The Judge had Tom kick him out of town. Quint was involved in a shooting right here at the Second Chance."

Springer said, "All right, Mister Quint. Tell us what you saw. Did Judge Mack pull his gun and shoot down Harold Higgins?"

"Sure did. Took his gun and held it aimed right at him and pull the trigger."

"Did the Judge have murder in his eyes?"

Quint grinned. "Sure did. Plain as day."

Jack muttered, "Objection, Orrie. Objection."

But Orrie said nothing.

Springer said, "Did Judge Mack come down the

stairs with murder in his eye, and shoot down the aforementioned Mister Higgins, while Mister Higgins' gun was still in his holster?"

"Yep. That's just the way it happened. I seen it with my own eyes."

"I can't take this any longer." Jack jumped to his feet and called out, "Objection! Leading the witness!"

Springer and everyone else looked at Jack.

He strode forward. "Mister Mortensen, members of the Town Council, I'm stepping in as attorney for Judge Mack."

Angie clapped her hands together "Yes! This is so exciting."

Springer glared at Jack. "You can't do that."

Mortensen looked at Aaron Digby, who was sitting beside him. "Can he do that?"

Digby shrugged his shoulders.

Springer looked at Mortensen. "No."

Jack stood in front of the Town Council. "Yes I can."

"You're forgetting a little thing called ethics, McCabe."

"When have ethics ever been a concern of yours?"

Judge Mack stood up. "Wait a minute. No one's asked me what I have to say about all this."

Mortensen leaned forward on his elbows. "What do you have to say about it, Judge?"

"Jack, I appreciate what you're doin'. But I don't take charity from no man."

Angie sprang to her feet. With her hands on her hips, she leaned forward, her brows dropped into a frown. "Now you listen to me, Judge Mack! Jack is gonna be your lawyer and that's the way it's gonna be. You understand me?"

The Judge gave a sheepish, "Yes, ma'am," and he sat back down.

Half of the crowd was laughing and the other half cheering. One man called out, "You tell 'em, Miss Angie!"

She looked back at them and gave a triumphant nod of her head.

Jack looked at Orrie. "Get out of the chair."

Orrie looked at Mack. "I still expect to be paid."

Mack said, "Get out of the chair, Orrie."

Orrie stormed out into the street, the barroom bursting with laughter.

Mortensen said, "Now, where were we?"

Jack looked at him. "I was filing an objection because our prosecutor was leading the witness."

Springer said, "This is not a court, McCabe."

Mortensen shrugged his shoulders. "Nathan's got a point."

"No, he doesn't." Jack began to pace back and forth. "We're here to determine the guilt of a man, if there is any, in the shooting death of another man. And if there is guilt, to determine to what degree."

He stopped pacing in front of Aunt Ginny. "And it benefits these proceedings not one whit to hear what the prosecuting attorney has to say. We have to hear what these witnesses have to say. In their own words."

Aunt Ginny nodded her head. "I agree."

A man somewhere behind Johnny said, "What's a *whit*?"

In Ginny's eyes was the glint of a smile. She was proud of her nephew.

Mortensen said, "All right. I guess the objection makes sense. What am I supposed to say, if I was a judge?"

Mack said, "Objection sustained."

"So be it." Mortensen tapped his gavel on the table. "Objection sustained."

Springer said to Jack, "You cannot simply bully your way into these proceedings like some sort of highway robber."

"You're welcome to file a complaint."

Mortensen tapped his gavel again. "Boys, let's get on with this. We don't have all day. I have a business to run."

Springer addressed his witness. "All right, Mister Quint. So the erstwhile Mister McCabe will not have a temper tantrum, please tell the Town Council, in your own words, what you saw?"

"I seen Judge Mack coming down the stairs with his gun drawn. That Higgins feller was at the foot of the stairs. I figger the Judge threw him down."

"Objection," Jack said.

Springer turned to him. "Oh, for heaven's sake, what for?"

"The witness is giving his opinion. He wasn't called in as an expert witness to give an opinion. He was called in as a material witness to tell us only what he saw."

Mortensen pounded his gavel on the table. "Objection sustained."

He looked at Aaron Digby. "I kind'a like this."

Springer rolled his eyes. "All right. Since we are playing courtroom games, Mister Quint, did Mister Higgins have a gun on his person?"

Quint looked at him as if to say, *Huh?*

"Was he wearing a gun?"

Quint nodded. "Oh. Yeah."

"Had Mister Higgins drawn his gun?"

Quint shook his head. "Nope. It was right there in his holster the whole time."

"Did Judge Mack say anything before he pulled the trigger?"

"Yep. He said, *Now you die.* And then he aimed his gun at him." Quint made a fist with his index finger extended, like Springer had earlier. "And then he shot him down like a dog."

Judge Mack shook his head. "Weren't the way of it."

Jack placed a hand on his arm to shush him.

Springer began striding back toward his table, and he glanced over at Jack. "Your witness."

Jack got to his feet. He had no notes to read from and had not prepared for this at all, but he knew what to do. He just had to make sure he did it well. After all, much of delivering an argument before a jury was timing and delivery. And even though no jury was present, he knew he had to treat the Town Council like a jury if he was to keep Judge Mack from being tried for murder.

"Mister Quint, what is your profession?"

Quint looked at him.

"What do you do for work?"

"Oh, I've done a lot of things. Cowhand, bronc buster, worked as a drover one summer. Done a lot of things."

"And what are you doing now for work?"

He shrugged. "I'm workin' for a land speculator."

Jack looked at him. "Do you even know what that means?"

He shrugged. "Don't really. It's what the boss says he is."

The crowd laughed.

Springer stood up. "Objection, relevance. What does any of this have to do with the shooting?"

Jack looked at Mortensen. "I'm just trying to establish the credibility of the witness."

Mortensen nodded his head. "I guess that sounds good. Objection...what would you say? Not sustained?"

Jack grinned. "Overruled."

Mortensen tapped his gavel down. "By gum, objection overruled."

Jack went back to the witness. "All right, Mister Quint, let's talk about the shooting."

"I done told everything I saw. Do I gotta tell it all again?"

More laughter.

Jack said, "Let's talk about what you said. According to the previous witness, Mister Higgins had drawn his gun before Judge Mack fired at him. But you said his gun was still in his holster."

"Uh..." Quint looked over at Hiram. "I never said that."

"Don't look at the other witness. Look at me. If you're just telling us what you saw, you don't have to look at anyone else."

"I know what I said and I didn't say what you said I said."

Myrna said, "Hate to tell you, Tootsie, but you did."

Lots of laughter.

"Miss Warren," Jack said, "could you read back for us the witness's exact words?"

She had already filled up two pages. She scanned down one page with her eyes and found what she was looking for. "Mister Springer asked, *Had Mister Higgins drawn his gun?* And you said, *Nope. It was right there in his holster the whole time.*"

Quint scratched his chin. "I said that?"

Jack nodded his head.

"How do we know that there girl got it right?"

"Believe me, if Miss Warren says you said it, you said it."

Quint shrugged his shoulders.

"So, Mister Quint, how do you explain the difference in your story and that of the other witness?"

Springer got to his feet. "Objection. Argumentative."

Mortensen said, "What does that mean?"

"It means he's harassing the witness."

"No, I want to hear the answer. Objection overruled. But make it quick, will you, Jack?"

Jack said to Quint, "Answer the question. How do you explain the differences in your stories?"

Quint shrugged his shoulders. "I don't know. A lot happened kind'a fast. If you blinked your eyes, you would have missed part of it."

Hiram piped up, "Maybe I was wrong about the gun."

Jack sighed. "All right. No further questions."

Springer stood. "I would now like to call to the witness stand the defendant. Judge Hannibal McIntyre."

Jack got to his feet. "Objection. A defendant has the right not to testify. In fact," he looked at the Judge, "I recommend not testifying, at least until I have time to consult with you."

"As has been pointed out already, this is not a court of law but a meeting of the Town Council. I would argue that Constitutional rights regarding testifying in court do not apply here."

Mortensen looked at Jack. "Gotta say, I think he has a point, Jack. Objection overruled."

Springer gave Jack a look as if to say, *Gotcha!*

Mack got to his feet and walked wearily to the witness chair and Hunter swore him in.

Springer said, "Can you give your name for the record?

"Already did."

Myrna said, "He did. I have it right here."

Springer looked annoyed. "Then let it show, for the record, that Judge Hannibal McIntyre has taken the stand."

Myrna's pencil was furiously scratching away.

Judge Mack folded his arms in front of him. "Don't like the name Hannibal. Never did."

Angie spoke up from Johnny's table. "I didn't know that was your first name until we had been dating for a whole month."

Chuckles spread throughout the crowd.

Mortensen pounded his gavel on the table. "Order in the court."

He looked at Aaron Digby. "I always wanted to say that."

Everyone laughed. Even Jack, in spite of himself. Except for Nathan Springer—he wasn't laughing. Jack wondered if he ever laughed.

Springer said, "Judge, could you please tell us the events that transpired yesterday afternoon at the Cattlemen's Club?"

"I done shot and killed a man that was being rough with Angie."

"Did you shoot him down in cold blood? Remember, Judge, you are under oath."

"I wouldn't call it cold blood."

"Then what would you call it?"

"I caught him forcing himself on Angie. I hit him a few times and then threw him down the stairs. Then I come down to keep on beating on him. He grabbed a gun Miss Maybelle was holding and I went for mine, and we both fired but I was a better shot."

"Did you fire first?"

He shrugged. "Hard to tell."

"Did you intend to kill him when you followed him down the stairs?"

"Didn't give it much thought. I was madder'n a cut snake."

"Would you have beaten him to death if you hadn't shot him?"

Mack shrugged his shoulders. "Ain't never beaten a man to death." Then he hesitated. "Well, I did once, but it was a long time ago and it was by accident."

Jack rolled his eyes.

Springer said, "Can you tell us about it?"

"Can, but I ain't gonna."

"Do I have to remind you that you are under oath?"

"I can tell you, in full honesty and under oath, that I ain't gonna tell you about it."

The barroom erupted in laughter again. Mortensen was too busy laughing to strike his gavel down on the table and call for order.

"One more question, Judge. You say Higgins fired at you."

The Judge nodded his head. "That's the way of it."

"But the previous witnesses stated there was only one shot fired."

"They was wrong."

The Judge looked at Springer. "What would you have done in my place, Springer? You find a man trying to force himself on the woman you love. What would you do?"

"Maybe consider fetching the marshal."

"Not if you're any kind of man."

One man called out from the back, "That's why you ain't married, Springer."

More laughter.

Springer walked away. "No further questions."

Mortensen looked at Jack. "Got any questions for him?"

Jack didn't know what line of questioning he could possibly pursue to undo the damage that had already been done. "No, I don't think so. But I would like to call Marshal Tom McCabe to the stand."

Springer said, "I haven't rested my case yet."

"As you have reminded us, this is not a court of law so the usual rules don't apply."

Aaron Digby said, "Jack, we all have businesses to run. This can't take all day."

"I just have to make a point. There's some discrepancy as to whether Mister Higgins fired his gun. I intend to prove that he did."

Tom walked over to the witness chair and Hunter swore him in.

Jack said, "Tom, did you inspect the gun of Mister Higgins?"

Tom nodded his head. "I inspected both guns. I have them both in my office."

"Had Mister Higgins fired his gun?"

Tom nodded again. "One shot had been fired from each gun, and I could tell by the smell of gunpowder and the fresh soot gunpowder leaves on the inside of a gun barrel that they had both been fired recently."

"How recently?"

"I would say within the hour of when I inspected them. Which was about an hour after the shooting."

Jack said to Springer, "Your witness."

Springer shook his head. "I have no questions."

Mortensen looked to Jack and then Springer. "All right. You boys both done?"

Jack nodded. "I suppose so."

Springer said, "For now."

Mortensen said, "All right, Marshal. I would appreciate it if you would take the prisoner back to jail while we toss this one over."

15

JUDGE MACK GOT to his feet and he and Tom headed
out to the street.

Mack glanced down at the handcuffs that were
still on over his wrists. "Are these really necessary?"

Tom shrugged. "It's a town ordinance."

They stepped down from the short boardwalk in
front of the Second Chance to the muddy street.

Mack looked at him. "You know these couldn't
stop me if I really wanted to cause trouble. And you
couldn't hold me in that cell unless I allowed myself to
be held."

Tom nodded. "I know your reputation, Judge. But
I hope you know mine."

"Boys," Angie said from behind them. "Hold up,
will you?"

She had followed them out from the Second
Chance.

Tom said, "Angie, I can't let a citizen walk with us.
Town ordinance. It has to be law officers, only."

"Oh, hang those town ordinances. I'm walking
with the Judge."

Tom shrugged, and the three continued walking
toward the jail.

Mack grinned. "You and I may be tough men with
reputations, but neither one of us could stand up to
her."

Angie said, "That's the truth."

Aunt Ginny said, "I don't think we have
established anything close to guilt beyond a shadow of a
doubt. Hiram McCabe's story is quite different from that
of this Quint fellow."

Springer said, "That happens, ma'am. Sometimes
an event transpires quickly and those not trained in
observation can miss crucial details, or even get them
wrong. I have seen witnesses differ on the color of a

man's hair."

Hiram stood. "I must say, I find this line of thought a little offensive. I know what I saw."

Johnny, still sitting at his table, said, "Sit down, Hiram."

Quint stood and looked back at Johnny. "Look, old man. We got a right to be here just as much as you."

"Sit down. Both of you. Ain't gonna tell you twice."

Springer sighed and shook his head. "Sit down, please."

They did.

Jack said to Springer, "Maybe the witnesses should leave. Otherwise, we could be here for hours trying to get this figured out."

Springer nodded. He looked to Quint and Hiram.

Quint said, "Have it your way. We'll be at the bar in the hotel."

Hiram followed him out the door.

Alisha Summers said, "Only one of them mentioned the gun of Mister Higgins had been fired. Why would the other one leave that out?"

Maybelle stood up. "May I speak?"

Mortensen waved a hand at her. "Please do. This is a meeting of the Town Council, and all residents of Jubilee are welcome to attend and offer comments."

"Well, I was there for the very end of it. I saw the Judge shoot."

Jack looked at her. "You were there?"

She nodded her head.

Jack said to Springer, "Why didn't you call her as a witness?"

She said, "I talked to Mister Springer and offered to be a witness but he said no."

Springer shook his head. "I didn't need her. I had full statements from the other two."

"*All* witnesses should have been brought forth," Jack said. "That is, if you were sincerely interested in getting to the truth."

"If you weren't so busy grandstanding and did

your preliminary studies of the case, you would have been aware that she was present at the time of the shooting. You could have called her as a witness."

Maybelle said, "I also didn't realize Higgins had fired his gun."

Aaron Digby said, "Could he have fired it at some point earlier in the day?"

Jack shook his head. "Tom is an experienced lawman and he knows guns. If he says a gun was fired within the hour, you can bank on that."

Springer stood ramrod straight, glaring at Jack. "And, of course, his name is McCabe, so we have to accept his statement as though he were God himself, because a McCabe could never be wrong."

Jack looked at him. "Is your problem with me or my entire family?"

"My problem is with anyone who holds themselves above the law."

He looked over at Johnny. "Last summer, in this very room, you beat a man to death and shot another."

Johnny shook his head. "Tom was right here the whole time. He called the killing justified."

"You're making my point, sir."

Johnny thought about that for a moment. "How's that?"

"I was down in Bozeman the day of the killings. In fact, I didn't return to Jubilee until three days later. I heard about the killings second hand, at the barber shop, a day after I returned. I went to see Marshal McCabe, then I came here to question any witnesses. It turns out we had a conspiracy of silence."

Johnny got to his feet. "One of those men shot down Mister Chen in cold blood. The other ordered it."

Sam Middleton was leaning against the bar. He had been silent until now. "And what would have happened? They were both part of the Chinese embassy. They had diplomatic immunity. They would have gone free."

Springer said, "It might not be fair, but it's the

law."

Johnny was still on his feet. "You want to put me on trial for murder, go right ahead."

Springer shook his head. "There's not a jury here who would convict you of anything. You're the legendary Johnny McCabe. The so-called Gunman of the Rio Grande, or whatever they call you. Putting you on trial would be a circus. And Chen was an old man who was well-liked."

Aunt Ginny said, wearily, "Mister Springer, what's your point?"

"My point is that I don't like it when society holds a man above the law, beyond justice, simply because he's famous."

Johnny said, "That's not the way of it with me."

"No? If your name weren't Johnny McCabe, would you have simply walked away from that incident last summer with no charges filed? Without at least an investigation?"

Johnny had nothing to say. He wanted to say Springer was just filled with small-minded pettiness. But he couldn't. He sat back down.

Mortensen tapped his gavel on the table. "Gentlemen, let's get back to the matter at hand. Is there enough evidence against Judge Mack to justify a charge of murder? Keep in mind we're not deciding whether or not he's guilty. Only if the matter should go to court."

"I believe it should indeed go to court," Springer said. "I recommend the Town Council vote in favor of charging Judge Mack with murder in the first degree."

Jack stepped forward. "And I ask the Town Council respectfully not to charge him as such. The Judge is of impeccable character, enough for Governor Potts to appoint him to a judgeship."

"Impeccable character?" Springer looked at Jack incredulously. "The man's a lunatic. His mind is whiskey-addled. He looks like some sort of wild man from the mountains. He's dating a woman young enough to be his daughter, and I suspect she's something of a simpleton."

"That's enough. There's no need to impugn her character."

"There is, if it shows the Judge's lack of character."

Aaron Digby said, "I don't know but maybe Mister Springer has a point, to some extent. I like the Judge well enough. I think we all do. I've shared a glass of whiskey or two with him right here at the Second Chance. But he is a man from a bygone era. There aren't many left like him, and those men defined the law themselves, by their own ability with a gun. But the West is becoming more civilized. Vigilante law is no longer necessary, and we have to remember as much as it might have been necessary at one time, it is actually against the law. And we are a nation of laws."

Jack shook his head. "And I think our prosecutor is letting his own anger at my father, and maybe a case of petty jealousy, motivate his intentions in this case. Motivating him to look for guilt when there is none."

Springer said, "Did you just call me petty?"

"I've called you worse."

No one was laughing.

Springer looked at Mortensen and Digby. "I'm sure the Judge is a likable enough fellow. I've never gotten to know him, myself. I find his boorish behavior offensive. But regardless of whether or not we like him," he turned and looked directly at Johnny, "the day of vigilante justice in this land is coming to an end. We need to make the statement that justice is dispensed in a court of law, not with the business end of a six gun."

Jack looked at the Council members one at a time as he spoke. "And I think we all need to focus on the matter directly at hand, which is yesterday's shooting, and not some larger agenda dealing with vigilante justice, or the prosecutor's anger at my father over the shootings last summer."

He turned his gaze to Springer. "Let such agendas

be determined by our politicians and by newspaper editorialists. A court of law should not be about larger agendas or editorializing. It should be about justice as defined by the law, and nothing else."

Mortensen let out a long sigh. "All right. Does anyone want to make a motion to charge Judge Mack with murder?"

One man in the back said, "I move that we let the Judge go, and we open the bar for drinks."

"Only Council members can make a motion."

"Oh."

The Council members were silent for a moment. Then Aaron Digby stood up. "As much as I like Judge Mack, I'm not really convinced one way or the other by anything that's been said here today. I say we should let a court of law figure it out. I move that we file charges against him."

A man Jack knew as Theodore Little stood up. He ran a small apothecary shop in town. "I second the motion."

Mortensen said, "I don't think this should be done by a showing of hands. I want individual votes. Aaron?"

Digby nodded his head. "Aye."

Aunt Ginny was next to Digby, and she said, "Nay."

Then it was Alisha Summers' turn. "Nay."

Tom unlocked the handcuffs and slid them from the Judge's wrists, then the Judge stepped into a cell and Tom closed the door and inserted a key and turned it.

"If it means anything, Judge, if I were in your place, I would've done the same thing."

"You still courtin' that little school marm?"

Tom nodded. "Hilly. Married her three years ago."

The Judge blinked with surprise. "You don't say. Well, when I come into town I'm either busy with court-related matters, or I'm otherwise occupied."

He looked at Angie with a grin.

She stood just outside the cell door, and she reached in through the bars to take his hand.

The Judge looked at Tom. "So what you're sayin' is if some yahoo started trying to force himself on Miss Hilly, you'd do what I done."

Tom nodded. "I'd break his neck. Or put a bullet in him."

Angie said to the Judge, "I don't want them to hang you, Sweetie. And I don't want you to rot in prison."

Tom said, "The Town Council might not vote to charge the Judge, Miss Angie."

"But they might."

"Even if they do, it doesn't mean he's going to prison. It just means he's going to trial." Tom slung the ring of keys over a peg on the wall. "Want some coffee, Judge?"

"Don't mind if I do."

Danny came in from walking rounds.

Tom said, "Any word yet from the Second Chance?"

Danny shook his head. "Not yet."

Tom glanced through the doorway to the cell block and saw Angie still standing in front of the Judge's cell. "Miss Angie, you really shouldn't be in there."

"I ain't goin' nowhere."

Tom sighed. He knew he wasn't going to win this one. "Danny, would you take a chair into the cell block for Miss Angie?"

"Is that allowed? What'll Mister Springer say?"

"He'll probably have a cow, but what's new? If it's not over this, it'll be something else."

Danny grabbed hold of a wing-back chair and toted it into the cell block for Angie. "Sorry, ma'am, this is the best we got."

When the coffee was ready, Tom filled two blue specked cups and brought them into the cell block. "Want some coffee, Miss Angie?"

"Oh, no thank you, Marshal. I ain't much of a coffee drinker."

Tom handed one cup through the bars to the Judge. "So, once this whole thing is over, how do you think your working relationship will be with our town prosecutor?"

Mack took a sip of coffee. "I think it might be time for me to leave this *judge* business behind. I've been a judge for a number of years now and it's growing tiresome." He looked at Angie. "I think it might be high time for you and me to get married and find some quiet corner of the Earth where we can settle down."

Her eyes were wide with wonder. "Are you really asking me to marry you, Judge?"

"Sure am, Sweetie. Will you?"

"Oh, yes. Yes, yes, yes, yes."

Tom watched with amazement. You would think the Judge had gotten down on one knee with a bouquet of flowers in one hand and made the most grand, romantic gesture, ever.

Angie looked at Tom. "Marshal, you gotta unlock this door so I can give the Judge the biggest hug and kiss he's ever gotten."

Tom shrugged his shoulders and reached for the ring of keys on the wall. Springer wouldn't like it, but Tom didn't care. He didn't work for Springer. Both he and Springer were employed by the Town of Jubilee and answered to the Town Council.

He unlocked the door and she went in and the Judge wrapped his arms around her and spun her around. She giggled and he laughed. And they kissed. And they hugged and kissed again.

Tom said, "All right, kids. This is not a honeymoon suite."

The Judge set Angie's feet back on the floor. "He's right, My Love. You gotta step back out so's he can lock the door again."

Jack stepped in the front door of the office. "That coffee smells good. Got any left?"

Danny sat at his desk. "Help yourself."

Jack grabbed a tin cup from a shelf of mismatched cups and filled it from the kettle, and he headed to the cell block.

The Judge said, "Tell me you've got good news."

Jack shook his head. "I wish I could. The Town Council voted five to four in favor of filing a murder charge."

Tom took a sip of coffee. "So, what's next?"

"Mister Mortensen will send a telegram to Governor White and tell him we need a judge appointed, at least for this trial."

"Could be weeks before the new judge gets here," Mack said.

Angie looked at him. "Oh, Judge. Whatever are we gonna do?"

"Just love each other, Sweetie. Nothing else we can do."

The Judge took a sip of coffee. "This is mighty good coffee, Marshal. Thank you."

Tom shrugged. "It's as good as jailhouse coffee gets, I suppose."

Mack grinned. "I suppose I've gotten used to jailhouse coffee over the years, from both sides of these bars."

He looked at Jack. "Counsellor, Miss Alisha is opening for business today and she'll need Angie. Could you walk her down to the Cattlemans'?"

Jack nodded his head.

As he walked down the boardwalk with Angie, she wiped away tears. "Oh, Jack. I'm so afraid. I don't want the Judge to hang or to spend the rest of his life in prison. I just couldn't live without him."

Jack didn't know quite what to think of Judge Mack or Miss Angie. She would sometimes go two or three months without seeing him, when he was presiding over court in other parts of the Territory that were assigned to him. But when they were together they were like young lovers who couldn't bear to be apart.

"I really don't think Springer has much of a case. Two witnesses can't agree on their statements. Miss Maybelle is a third witness, and she disagrees with the other two. If not for Springer doggedly pursuing this, I doubt there would have been a murder charge at all. The problem is Springer. He's angry at my father—the entire family, in fact—and he's taking it out on the Judge. I don't think Springer has much of a case at all, so I wouldn't worry too much. The hard part will be for the Judge, waiting in jail for the new judge to arrive."

"Can't we get him out on bail?"

Jack shrugged his shoulders. "To get bail set, we have to have an arraignment, and for that we need a judge."

They stopped at the front door of the Cattleman's. At least Angie's tears had stopped. "Well, I don't know about all this lawyer talk, but I trust you. The Judge says you're the best he's ever seen."

And with that, she headed inside.

Jack headed back to the office. Myrna had returned ahead of him. "No appointments today, Boss."

He nodded his head. "Maybe I'll just head home this afternoon. This case is giving me a lot to think about."

"Seems to me it should be open-and-shut."

"Should be hardly worth the prosecutor's time."

He glanced at a clock mounted on one wall. It was three minutes to one. A little early in the day for a beer, but he found himself thinking about one, anyway. "I think I'll head over to the Second Chance before I go home."

He walked along the boardwalks, his hands in his pockets. He was in a jacket and tie, with a Stetson pulled down over his temples. He was not wearing a gunbelt, as he thought it might send the wrong impression to potential clientele, like he was trying to capitalize on his father's fame. After all, even though Jack had long since left behind the feeling that he was somehow lost in his father's shadow, he wanted to build a life on his own merit.

The saloon half of the Second Chance once again looked as it usually did. The bar was open, and the tables were all back where they had been before this morning's meeting of the Town Council.

Three cowhands were at a table, laughing and sharing some mugs of beer. Must be working at the old Willbury place, Jack figured. A man Jack knew only as Long was at the bar. Hair down to his shoulders and a bushy beard. He wore a buckskin shirt that was kind of long, like a smock, and a belt tied it down across the middle. A knife was sheathed at his right side—looked at first glance like it might be a Bowie. Tucked into the front of the belt and turned backwards for a cross draw was a Colt revolver.

Long had a glass of whiskey in front of him. He nodded his head at Jack. "McCabe."

Jack nodded back at him. "Long. Were you here this morning for the festivities? I didn't see you in the crowd."

Long shook his head. "Here in town to try and sell some beeves. But Hunter's been telling me about it. Sounds like I missed a real circus."

Hunter walked over and Jack said to him, "You have any cold beer?"

A new boy was working for Hunter. He was skinny and with a mop of wild hair. Jack knew him as Milton but didn't know his last name. Or if Milton *was* his last name.

Hunter called over to him. "Hey, Milton! Climb down and fetch Mister McCabe a cold beer."

Milton had a broom in his hands. He set it down and headed for the root cellar.

Long said, "I met Judge Mack once, down on the border. We almost drew on each other. But then afterwards we wound up sharing a bottle of whiskey."

Jack looked at him with a little surprise. "Someday you're gonna have to tell me how a man who runs a small cattle ranch looks like a gunfighter and has a past that includes men like Judge Mack."

Long grinned. "No I ain't."

He took a sip of whiskey. "Besides, look at your father. He's a cattleman but also one of the best known gunfighters there is. And even you. Duded up like a fancy lawyer, which I suppose you are, but you carry yourself like you can handle yourself. And you got steel in your eye."

Milton brought a mug of beer that was cold enough to be already producing a layer of fine mist on the outside of the glass. "Here you go, Mister McCabe."

Jack nodded his thanks and took a sip. "So, Long, did you get to know the Judge well enough to know if he would be capable of murder?"

"He's a hard man. Them days required hard men. But I don't believe he would shoot a man down in cold blood. If you're capable of that kind of thing and do it, you develop a bad reputation real quick. The Judge was always known as a hard man you didn't want to cross, but he was a stand-up sort of man."

"Would you be willing to testify to that in court, as a character witness, if it comes to that?"

Long shrugged. "I suppose so."

Long finished his remaining whiskey in one gulp. "I'll see you gentlemen later. I got me some beeves to sell."

When he was gone, Jack leaned one elbow against the bar and he took a deep swallow of beer. "I got a bad feeling about this trial."

Hunter was behind the bar. "Why's that? You think the Judge might be guilty?"

Jack shook his head. "No, I agree with Long's assessment of him."

Hunter nodded. "Me too. I've met back-stabbers and cold blooded murderers over the years. The Judge ain't one of 'em."

"I've got a feeling something else is going on here. I just don't know what. But I'll figure it out. I have to. The Judge's life might depend on it."

Hiram McCabe sat at a table in the hotel lounge with a glass of scotch in front of him. His father had often said not to sit with your back to the door. But Hiram didn't want to see the door. He didn't even want to see people coming in or going out. He didn't really want to see life happening around him at all. What he wanted was to find a hole somewhere and go crawl into it and be left alone.

He heard Quint's whiskey-soaked voice from the doorway. "There you are!"

Hiram cringed.

Quint half shuffled, half danced his way over to Hiram's table. Hiram didn't know if Quint was drunk or just out of his mind. He didn't really care.

"Ain't you gonna ask me where I've been?"

Hiram shook his head. "No."

Quint called over to the bar. "Hey, barkeep! Bring me over a glass. And a bottle."

The bartender was a small man with thin wisps of hair combed over a balding head. He brought over a bottle of whiskey and a glass and set them on the table.

Quint grabbed the bottle and then slid out a chair and dropped into it. "Come on. Ask me."

Hiram shook his head, not even looking at the man.

"All right, I'll tell you. Used to be the whore house in this town was Miss Alisha's. But she's done become a legitimate business woman and opened up a restaurant."

"I know." Hiram gave a weary sigh. "That's where we were yesterday, when we witnessed the killing we lied about under oath."

"Oh, yeah. That's right." Quint slid aside the glass and pulled a drink right from the bottle. He shook his head and let out a whiskey-soaked breath that made Hiram pull back in his chair. "Yessir, that ain't bad hooch."

He stood the bottle on the table. "So, anyway, I

decided to see if anyone else had taken Miss Alisha's place. And sure enough, there is."

Hiram shook his head. "Nature abhors a vacuum."

Quint was picking up the bottle again. "What's that about a whore? Yeah, I was looking for one. And I found Miss Dixie Longstreet runs what you might call an establishment further up Randall Road. Just beyond the town line. Turns out there's a new town ordinance ag'in whorin'. But it was sure worth the walk."

Hiram closed his eyes with disgust. "Please spare me the sordid details."

Quint took another chug from the bottle and wiped his mouth with the back of his sleeve. "So, tell me, what'd you find out?"

"The Town Council voted to file murder charges."

Quint nodded his head. "Good. That's what we wanted. So, what's next?"

"Next we have to wait for the governor to appoint another judge and send him out."

"How long will that take?"

"Could be weeks." He drained his whiskey glass. "Weeks that I will have to spend in this town."

Quint shrugged his shoulders. "That's all right. It'll give me time to harass the folks out at the McCabe Ranch. See if I can make their lives miserable."

"I thought at least part of our job in this town was to try and convince my uncle Johnny to sell."

Quint shook his head. "Not really. My job here is really to hurt 'em. To hurt 'em bad. I always do what Mister Randall tells me, and he said he wants me to make McCabe blood pour across the land like a river. And that's what I intend to do."

PART TWO

16

Two Weeks Later

EMMA McCABE HAD FINISHED HELPING Jessica clean up the kitchen after breakfast, and she took a book out onto the front porch. Pa had ridden out with Dusty and Charles a couple of hours earlier, planning to devote the day to cutting trees for firewood. Bree was out back with the herd, settling into her job as wrangler.

Em was twenty-two years old and unmarried, and she was in no hurry to change that status. Friends she knew were married. Mary-Kate had a baby girl that was a year and a half old. Clara Jenkins had married a young man who worked in the mines and they had a little one on the way. But Em was happy to live here at the ranch, to work alongside Jessica and Cora cooking, keeping house and chasing after Caleb and Beth. The twins were seven. Caleb wanted to climb trees and he couldn't wait to be old enough to ride out with the men in the morning, and Beth was helping in the kitchen, as much as a seven year old could.

Em was content with her life as it was. She was in no hurry for changes. No dreaming about things she didn't have.

"You have the soul of a poet," Aunt Ginny had said to her.

Em was not overly tall but not quite short. Her hair was the color of corn silk and at the moment it was tied in a bun behind her head. A blue shirt and a dark skirt completed the picture, as she took the rocker that was usually reserved for Aunt Ginny and opened her book.

The title was *Little Women* by Louisa May Alcott, who was becoming Em's favorite writer. Aunt Ginny had given her this book and she was now beginning her fourth run through it.

A mountain breeze drifted toward her, bringing with it the usual scent of balsam. She could also smell the earth in front of the porch, still a little damp from the night before.

She had liked living in the cabin at the rim of the small canyon north of the valley, but she liked living here at the main ranch house even better.

Her gaze landed on the first page of the book. The first chapter was titled PLAYING PILGRIMS.

"Christmas won't be Christmas without my presents," grumbled Jo, lying on the rug.

Em liked the name Jo for a girl. Short for Josephine. Em kind of wished her name was Jo.

Her name was actually Melissa Jean Pike, though she used the name McCabe. Seemed the proper thing to do, since Pa and Ma—Johnny and Jessica—had taken her in to raise as their own.

Pa had started calling her M.J., which Uncle Joe had shortened to just Em. Folks around town began calling her Emma, thinking that was the name that *Em* was short for, and most of them knew her as Emma McCabe. Pa had said it might be best not to correct them. Em's late father had an aunt who was trouble and might still be trying to find her, but the old woman would be looking for Melissa Jean Pike, not Emma McCabe. She liked the name Emma McCabe, though she kind of wished her name was Jo McCabe.

Cora came out onto the porch. She had dark hair, also tied into a bun, and she wore a white blouse and dark skirt. She was sixteen, a little shorter than Em. Ma's daughter by birth and Pa's by adoption. Though, in this family, adoption didn't matter. You became family by love, not by being born into it.

Cora stood, half-dancing and half-fidgeting as she shifted from one foot to the other. "I'm bored. Bored, bored, bored."

Em looked up at her. "What would you think if my

name was Jo?"

Cora took a sort of waltzing dance step toward the edge of the porch and placed her hands on a post that held up the small roof overhead. "I want to see the world. I want to dance with fine gentlemen and have them want to court me. I want to play coy and shy, and at other times be bold and daring. I want to see Paris. I want a young, French gentleman with too much money to propose to me, and I want to say, *I will need time to think about it, monsieur.*"

"Aunt Ginny says I have the soul of a poet. Ma says I should try writing. Do you think I should?"

Cora turned to face her. "How can you just sit there with a book and have no desire to venture past this ranch, when there is a whole world out there, just waiting to be seen. Just beckoning to us."

"I wonder if I could use Jo as a *name de plume*? I could take Aunt Ginny's last name. I could be Jo Middleton. Or Josephine Middleton. Or I could use the initials J.M, after the character in this book. Jo March. I could be J.M. Middleton. What do you think?"

Cora made a face like she thought Em was crazy. "Who wants to write when you can *live*?"

"I want to write about life."

"Life should be lived. Not written about."

Em shrugged her shoulders. "Maybe some of us are meant to go out into the world and embrace life, and others are meant to write about it."

Cora rolled her eyes and turned away.

Her tone changed. "Em!"

Em had just gone back to her book and now she looked up. There was alarm in Cora's tone. "What?"

Cora looked back to her. "There's a man! Out there! At the edge of the field, near the woods."

Em sprang out of the rocker and followed Cora's gaze to the woods to the west, near the end of the huge grassy meadow that made up this end of the valley. Far enough away that she had to squint to really see it, but she could make out a man standing at the edge of the trees.

"What do you think he's doing there?" Cora sounded scared.

"He's watching the house, is what he's doing." Em tossed her book to the rocker. It slid along the seat and fell through the opening between the seat and the back and landed on the floor. She would retrieve it later. "Go tell Ma what's going on. I'm gonna go tell Bree."

Em grabbed her skirt to lift the hem a couple of inches so she wouldn't trip over it, and she skipped down the front steps and ran to the side of the house, where Bree was showing Caleb how to spin a lariat.

"Bree!"

Bree and Caleb both looked over at her.

"There's a man. Standing at the edge of the great meadow, just watching the house."

"Where?"

Em pointed her finger to where the man was standing. "There."

Except he wasn't there anymore.

"Well, he *was* there, just a minute ago. I swear. Cora saw him, too."

"I'll saddle up and go check it out."

Caleb looked up at Bree. He wore a wide-brimmed hat that had gone floppy over the years. It had been Josh's, when Josh was a young boy growing up on this ranch. The rope was still in his hands. "I'll go with you, Bree."

"No, you stay here. You have to keep Em and Cora safe. And your Ma and Beth."

He nodded. "I'll do it. I'm a McCabe man."

Bree couldn't help but smile. "You sure are, Sweetie."

Bree put two fingers to her mouth and let out a long, shrill whistle, and the horse she called Flame lifted her head from where she had been grazing out in the meadow and trotted over.

Bree was in a range shirt and jeans, and the gun Aunt Ginny had given her for Christmas years ago was in a holster at one hip. Most women Em knew would be horrified at the thought of wearing trousers—those were garments for a man, and this was a time when a woman simply didn't wear clothes designed for a man. Em had never worn pants. And yet, Bree somehow did not look mannish in them.

Bree's hair was in a long, single braid that fell down along her back, and a flat-brimmed hat was pulled down over her temples. She had found a bun just didn't work well with a range hat, so she had taken to wearing a single braid.

She didn't take the time to lead Flame to the stable to be saddled. She just leaped up onto the back of the horse and rode off bareback toward where Em had seen the rider. She hadn't even taken the time to fashion a halter for Flame. She could turn the horse with a simple nudge of one knee or the other against the horse's shoulder.

Jessica came scurrying out the kitchen door, and Em told her what was happening.

"Go get the scattergun, Em. And whatever gun you want for yourself."

"Do you think there'll be trouble?"

Jessica's gaze was on Bree, who was now almost halfway to the edge of the meadow. "I hope not. But I've seen too much not to be prepared. Hurry, now. Go get the guns."

Em lifted her hem a couple of inches again and ran to the front porch. By the scattergun, Em knew Jessica wanted the twenty gauge double-barrel that stood in the rifle rack. Em's choice was the .32 caliber rifle Pa had bought a couple of years ago.

The guns were both loaded, but Em checked to make sure, anyway. Pa had said to always do that. Pa kept the guns loaded because he said a gun that's not loaded is of no use to anyone. He said keep your guns loaded and treat them like they're loaded.

She brought the scattergun out to Jessica and then stood with the Winchester .32 in her own hands, watching as Bree approached the edge of the meadow.

Strands of hair had pulled free from Em's bun and flew across her face, and she turned her head to make them fall away.

She wondered, as she stood with her rifle, if she would have the nerve to actually shoot at a man. If she had the nerve so many McCabes seemed to have. And if her hands would be steady enough to get off a shot that counted.

Bree brought Flame to a stop at the edge of the woods and began cutting for sign. Within three minutes she found the section of grass the man had been standing on.

She glanced back toward the house. She had a good view of the structure, and also the barn, the bunkhouse, and the grassy area out back where the remuda grazed. She could see the porch and the overhanging roof, but she couldn't tell if anyone was on the porch or not. She figured whoever had been standing here had seen Em bolt from the porch and decided it was prudent to ride away.

She wondered who he was, and what he wanted. You don't just stand and watch a house unless you want something. And she couldn't imagine any possible reason that might be good.

She decided to find out. His tracks were visible where he had headed back to the woods. Grass was matted down where he had walked, and in places she could see a distinctive boot print.

She drew her pistol and checked the loads, and she turned her horse into the woods to follow the trail.

The trees were mostly pine and separated by twenty feet or more. No underbrush impeded her, and she found the man's trail easy to follow. She saw where he had tethered the horse about fifty feet in from the meadow.

After he had mounted up, he rode toward the trail that would come out in town behind Hunter's.

The trail was rocky and uneven, and she knew she wouldn't be able to push her horse at much more than a walking speed. Neither could the man, but he had at least a ten minute lead on her. She wouldn't catch him.

She turned her horse back toward the ranch house, and she found Jessica and Em waiting for her—Jessica with her scattergun and Em with her rifle.

Bree said, "I knew there was no way I could catch him on that trail."

Jessica let her gaze travel to the edge of the woods. "I wonder who he was."

Em looked scared. "I wonder if he'll be back. What'll we do?"

Bree said, "We'll be ready for him."

17

JOHNNY SAT at the table listening to Bree tell him about the man who had been watching the ranch.

On a cattle ranch, you ate a lot of beef, and Jessica had learned various ways to prepare it. Tonight's dinner was a T-bone with wild onions and diced tomatoes, and a sauce that had bourbon as its primary ingredient.

"Dang good," Johnny had said, after his first bite of steak.

Bree and Charles were having dinner with them, and Charles had said, "Jessica, you are an artist when it comes to cooking.

Jessica served red wine with the steak. The wine was called *merlot*, and Johnny had learned years ago from Ginny that the T was silent. It didn't rhyme with *thought*, it rhymed with *throw*. Even though he would pronounce it wrong sometimes just to irritate her.

Johnny didn't have any wine, though. He was not one to want flavorful drinks when he ate. He had a tall glass of cold water, fresh from the well. Tonight, with Charles, he might have a glass of scotch. But with the meal, especially a steak this good, he wanted water only.

Bree was talking with the method women seemed to have of talking while eating, and yet never talking with their mouths full. Jessica could do it too, and so could Ginny. Johnny had noticed Em and Cora had both somehow mastered it. He remembered Lura could do it. He never could, though. You chewed and swallowed, then you talked. As such, he found it challenging to get a word in at this table. He noticed Charles seemed to have the same problem.

Bree ate and talked. "I was thinking about maybe following the rider, but along that rough trail, I knew I'd never catch up to him. He had a solid ten-minute start."

Johnny swallowed some steak and followed it with a chug of water. "I'm glad you didn't follow him. You've gotta figure, someone bold enough to stand out there and watch the ranch, in plain sight, is either really stupid or really smart. If he's really smart, there are half a dozen places along that trail to set up an ambush."

Bree looked at him. "I hadn't thought of that."

"In a way, I'm glad you didn't. I don't want any children of mine to live the kind of life where you have to learn to think like that."

Jessica took a sip of wine. "Who could it be? Who would want to just watch this ranch?"

Johnny was silent a moment.

Bree said, "What're you thinking, Pa?"

"I'm thinking about ten or eleven years ago, when those raiders hit this ranch. Vic Falcone isn't the same man that he was back then. At that time, if you had told me he would become a farmer living here in the valley and volunteering to help at church, I would have said you were out of your mind. But back then, it was a whole different situation. And it began with him having this ranch watched."

"I remember it all too well. You had Aunt Ginny and me hide in the root cellar under this kitchen. You gave me a gun and told me to shoot us both if the raiders got through the defense you had set up. I was only fifteen. I'll be honest with you, I didn't know if I had what it takes to do that."

"I'm glad you don't know and I hope you never do. But that was a desperate time. You know what they say. Desperate times call for desperate measures."

Em said, "Where does that expression come from?"

"Probably someone who knows what it's like to have raiders attacking his home."

Beth and Caleb were at the table, listening to every word. Some folks had the belief that hard topics should not be discussed in front of children, but Johnny thought they had to learn the way of the world, and what better way than here with family. To shield them and let them discover the hard realities later in the form of a rude awakening struck him as unfair.

"Maybe I'll ride into town tomorrow and talk with Tom. Since the rider took the trail that comes out behind the Second Chance, he might be staying in town. I might have a talk with Marvin, too. He's still working at the livery. Maybe the man in question rented a horse."

Jessica nodded her head. "I have a lot to do tomorrow, but maybe I'll go into town with you. I need to buy some fabric."

Em said, "I'll go into town for you, if you'd like. I know what fabric you want."

"Em, that would make my life so much easier."

Charles gave it a quick thought. "Pa, you and me and Dusty were planning to ride the fence line tomorrow, to make sure no more of it had been cut, but I'm sure Dusty and I can handle it."

"No, I want to ride along, too. Let's leave at sunrise, as soon as Dusty gets here." Pa looked at Em. "I should be back around noon. We'll head into town then."

"Great. And while we're there, I'll visit Aunt Ginny and see if she has any new books I could borrow."

Cora grinned. "Do I sense an ulterior motive?"

That got a chuckle from around the table.

Jessica said, "Johnny? Do you think that mysterious man today has anything to do with the fence that was cut?"

He shrugged his shoulders. "It's a possibility."

Cora looked concerned. "Do you think we're safe here, when you're off doing ranch business?"

"Bree will be here in the morning. A man would have to be a fool to tangle with her. And Dusty and Charles will be here in the afternoon while Em and I are in town. You'll be safe enough."

It was dark outside, and Hiram sat on the bed in his hotel room with the newspaper. It was a two-day old paper out of Helena but it was as close as this little cattle and mining town got to relevant news.

Hiram had read it twice, already. Oh, what he would give for an actual book. But he didn't know where to find one in this little town. There was no public library, and the general store didn't have books in stock. They were more concerned with carrying items the local ranchers and farmers might need in their livelihood. Dung forks, axes and shovels. But try to read a dung fork for some late night reading before bed, Hiram thought. You won't get very far.

With the kerosene lamp on the wall turned up and casting a pale light throughout the room, he sat at the edge of the bed with the newspaper. His tie was off and the top button of his shirt undone, and he sat with his legs crossed and the paper in his hands.

A wayward traveler had left a dog-eared Bible behind, and even though Hiram had little use for religion, he was so desperate for reading material he thought he might actually open it up.

The door handle rattled. Someone was out in the hallway, attempting to come into the room but finding the door locked. Hiram figured it had to be Quint. Any civilized person would have knocked at the door.

He got to his feet and walked wearily across the room. He slid back the dead bolt and opened the door and found it was indeed Quint.

The man pushed past Hiram and almost danced his way into the room. "I done it! I done it real good!"

Hiram rolled his eyes. "What? Did you find another whorehouse?"

"I rode out to the McCabe ranch, today. Not all the way out, but you know that little trail out behind the Second Chance?"

Hiram knew of no such trail.

Quint continued anyway. "I follered it all the way into the valley. Comes out onto this big, grassy field, and there's the ranch house, right in the middle of the field. So I thought I'd just stand there and watch the house for a while and make 'em nervous."

Hiram shook his head. "Those people don't get nervous. They get cautious, or they get angry. Or both. But they don't scare easily."

"Some young filly ran from the front porch to another one working by the corral. Figured I'd been seen and I knew I'd better get out of there, so I mounted up and rode back to town."

"You could have gotten yourself killed."

Quint grinned. "But I didn't, did I? I think them people ain't as tough as they're made out to be. Too many people listen to the legend. No one's as good as they claim Johnny McCabe is."

Hiram nodded wearily. "Yes, he is."

"Well, tomorrow I'm turning up the flames on that whole bunch. I hired two men to lean heavy on 'em. If they find one of the women alone, they're to give her a scare. Meanwhile, I'll be riding out to the valley again."

"You're going to get both of us killed, you know that?"

Quint shook his head with a grin. "You city fellers scare too easily. One of the things Mister Randall wants me to do is make their lives hard. No reason I can't have me some fun while I'm doing it."

Quint glanced about the room. "Got a bottle here?"

"No I don't. I finished it, with your help."

"I'm heading downstairs for one." And Quint was out the door.

Hiram looked at the empty doorway for a moment, wondering again how he had ever allowed himself to be caught up in a situation like this.

He wanted to go back to reading. He had always found reading relaxed him. But the newspaper no longer seemed adequate. He reached to a night stand beside the bed, and grasped the dog-eared Bible.

18

HE RODE into the valley from the flat grasslands east of it.

He was about thirty years old, with a range shirt that was now covered in dust, and blue trousers with a yellow cavalry stripe down each side, and black boots that rose to the knee. At his right side was an old Army holster with the flap cut away so he could have easier access to his gun. And his gun, like his holster, pants and boots, was Army issue. A colt single action .45 caliber.

Pulled down tightly about his temples was a Stetson that had been stiffly blocked at one time but was now losing its shape and its brim sagged a bit in front.

He had two canteens on his saddle, a bedroll and a pair of saddlebags tied to the cantle, and tucked into the saddle boot was a Spencer rifle.

He was due in Jubilee, and he probably should have taken the train like most people did these days. But he didn't like the train. Didn't like stagecoaches, either. During his time in the cavalry he had developed a love for riding through open country. And so, even though he had to travel from Cheyenne north to Jubilee, he did so on the back of a horse.

He thought by the shape of the ridges ahead there might be a pass into what he had heard was a valley. He would cut through it rather than around and shave off a few hours from his journey.

He hoped to be in Jubilee by evening. He wanted to settle in before he began his new job. He had served as an assistant to another man doing this job, but he had never done the job on his own.

"You'll do fine," his mentor had told him.

He hoped the old man was right.

It was while he was riding through the pass that his horse threw a shoe.

He swung out of the saddle and took a look at the hoof. The shoe had completely fallen off. Two nails had broken, and it looked like two had never been used at all. *Well, that's quality work,* he thought with a little sarcasm. It was what he got for not inspecting the work himself.

"Looks like we gotta walk," he said to the horse.

He had learned during his years in the cavalry that horses were smarter than they were often given credit for. You never knew just how much a horse understood, so he talked to his horses.

Looked like the horse was favoring its leg a little. Probably stepped down wrong when the shoe came off.

He took the reins and began walking, leading the horse behind him.

After an hour of walking, with dust and sweat mixing to form streams of grime down his face, he saw a two-floor log house in the distance. A barn stood nearby, and a longer, low-roofed structure he figured was probably a bunk house. It was all surrounded by luxuriant, green grass, which meant there was a good water supply. He had drained one canteen already and the other was almost empty.

He led his horse through the grass toward the house. As he got closer, he could see horses grazing out behind the house. He could also see a corral a ways off from the house and a woman standing by the fence with her gaze fixed on the single horse behind the fence.

Her hair was light blonde and tied up in a bun. As he got closer, he could tell she was a young woman. She was in a white blouse and a dark skirt, and she was leaning with her elbows on the top rail of the fence.

Once he was within shouting distance, he called out, "Hello the corral!"

She turned, startled. And he could see she was beautiful. He found her so captivating he almost stopped in his tracks.

"I didn't mean to startle you. My horse threw a shoe, and it's been a long walk. I was wondering if I could water him and refill my canteens."

She looked at him like she wasn't sure. "I don't know."

"I'm not here to cause any trouble." He shook his head. "My name is James Colter, and I'm due in Jubilee to start a job."

He had stopped a few yards from her, and from behind him he heard the sound of a gun's hammer being hauled back and clicking into place.

Another girl spoke. "That's far enough. Keep your hands where I can see 'em or I'll blow your head off."

He raised his hands to shoulder height. "Friendly in these parts, aren't you?"

"We've had trouble," the first girl said to him.

"You don't say."

"Drop that gun," the girl from behind him said.

He glanced over his shoulder at her. She didn't look much older than the first one, but her hair was dark and she was in a range shirt and had a blacksmith's leather apron tied on over what looked like jeans. He had never seen a woman wear trousers before.

What caught his gaze the most was the revolver in her hand. It was aimed at him and her aim seemed steady. From his experience in the cavalry, he knew a fighter when he saw one.

"Sorry, ma'am. I don't throw my gun down for anyone. All I want is to water my horse and refill my canteens. But maybe I picked the wrong place to stop at. Maybe I should just be on my way."

The blonde girl said, "What job are you taking in Jubilee?"

He touched the brim of his hat. "The Reverend James Colter, at your service. I'm the new Methodist minister."

"Emma McCabe. Pleased to meet you."

Bree huffed a sigh of aggravation. "Em, don't go telling him your name."

The man nodded. "McCabe. Should've figured. I've heard your family has a ranch in this area."

"I don't want to just shoot a man down. So you get moving. Don't let us see you around here again."

A man spoke, from off near the side of the barn. "Get moving."

Colter glanced over his shoulder. The man was sitting on a horse near the barn. He had a wide-brimmed hat shading his face, and he was dressed in range clothes, but what Colter noticed most was the revolver in his hand.

"Johnny McCabe, I presume?"

"I won't miss at this distance."

Bree said, "Neither will I."

Colter nodded his head. "Well, I would hate for you all to waste lead on me, so I'll be moving on. Can you tell me where Jubilee is from here?"

Em said, "Down the trail along the valley floor. When you see another trail break off to the left, through a pass, take it. Then another left and follow it into town. It's three miles. There's a trail off in that direction," she nodded her head toward the edge of the woods west of the meadow. "It's considerably shorter but much harder going. Might be too hard on your horse with his sore leg."

Colter touched the brim of his hat again. "Thank you, Miss McCabe."

He began walking toward the trail that cut across the valley, leading his horse behind him.

Walking toward the trail brought him past Johnny, and Colter glanced at him. "Pleasure to meet you, sir."

"Keep on walking."

Johnny rode up to the corral and swung out of the saddle. Bree walked on over, her revolver now holstered.

They watched as the man stopped at the bridge that crossed a small creek. Instead of leading his horse across the bridge, he led it down to the water. Then he removed a canteen from his saddle, pulled the cork and pushed the canteen down into the water. Once his canteen was full, he grabbed a second one and did the same.

Em kept her gaze on him. "He said he was the new minister."

Johnny shook his head. "That man's no minister. He's a gunfighter."

19

JOHNNY HAD INTENDED to take the buckboard to town, but Em said, "No, Pa, I'd rather we saddle up. I've been in the mood to go riding all morning, but Ma and Bree thought it might be too dangerous because of that man yesterday."

Bree, as the wrangler, fetched them two horses and saddled them, and Johnny and Em mounted up.

Johnny said to Em. "Let's take the long way to town. It's almost three miles longer, but the back trail has too many places for an ambush."

"You'd take the back trail if you were riding alone, wouldn't you? Or if Bree was with you."

Johnny nodded. "Bree's a gunfighter, or as close to it as any woman I have ever known. I sometimes call her a lady gunhawk. But that doesn't mean you aren't capable. You shouldn't measure yourself in comparison to others."

"You sound like Aunt Ginny."

He grinned. "I'm not sure how to take that."

Em laughed and they rode along.

She might not be a lady gunhawk, Johnny thought, but she rode naturally, moving with the horse like she and the horse were one.

"So," he said. "I understand you're having thoughts about being a writer."

Em looked at him with surprise. "How did you know? I haven't mentioned it to anyone."

Johnny grinned. "I'm a man of mystery."

"No. Seriously. How did you know?"

"Aunt Ginny told me. She has known writers over the years. Mostly back in 'Frisco. She said you have that certain way a writer does."

Em's gaze went to the trail ahead of them. "Do you think I could do it? Be a writer?"

"I don't know much about such things, but your Uncle Matt is much better read than I am and more familiar with the various arts. He has said you don't really become a writer, or for that matter, a painter or a sculptor. You just are one. And I think you might indeed be a writer."

"Do you think I could really do it? I mean, write a book? Do you think people might read my book? Young women might read about my characters, like I read about those by Louisa May Alcott?"

He shrugged. "I don't know much about the writing business, but it seems to me it's probably like any other business. You learn to do it, and once you're good enough, then you're good enough."

"But you do think I might have writing talent?"

He shrugged again. "Don't know much about talent, either. But it seems to me anything you have a passion for, if you're willing to do the work and learn how to do it, you'll be good at it."

"Aunt Ginny says everyone has talent, of one kind or another. What's your talent?"

"Well, I know horses and cattle. I can read sign. It's been said I'm one of the better trackers around. You're Uncle Joe said that, and he's about the best tracker I ever saw." He shrugged one more time. "And I suppose I'm good with a gun. Better'n I probably should be. It's gotten me into trouble more times than I care to remember."

They followed the trail to where another trail broke off to the left, just as she had described to the man who had claimed to be the new minister. They followed it through the pass known as McCabe Gap, the same name the little community that predated Jubilee had been called. Then they turned left onto Willbury Road.

That was where they passed the gunfighter, who was still on foot leading his horse. He waved at them and Johnny nodded, but he and Em kept moving.

As they rode, Em glanced over her shoulder at him.

"Pa, what do you think of him?"

"Like I said, that man's a gunfighter."

"How can you tell? Because he wears a gun? A lot of men wear a gun."

"It's more about the way he carries himself. The way he reacted when I spoke. The way he didn't look frightened to know Bree and I were aiming guns at him. That man has had guns aimed at him before. Probably been shot at more than once. I had the feeling the reason he didn't go for his gun wasn't because he was afraid to, but because he chose not to."

"Well, he had two guns aimed at him. He couldn't go for his gun or he would've gotten shot."

"Not necessarily. I've been in that position a couple of times. Both times I shot my way out of it. But there's another reason, too. I was sitting there for a couple of minutes before I said anything, and I heard him say he doesn't throw his gun down for anyone."

"That's the kind of thing a gunfighter would say?"

Johnny nodded. "It's the kind of thing *I* would say."

Quint stood on the front porch of the hotel. The Methodist Church was to his right, where Willbury Street met Randall at a right angle. Straight ahead and across Willbury was the Second Chance, and he had a good view of the marshal's office, down the street a ways.

In his teeth was clenched a cigar, and he leaned with one shoulder against a post that held up a roof overhead.

Two men stood with him. One wore a miner's hat that was called a kepi but was starting to be called a cap. He had a gun tucked into the front of his belt and a long knife sheathed at his left side. The other man was in a range shirt and buckskin pants, and he wore a gun holstered at his right side and a knife sheathed in one boot. Neither of the two men had bathed since the last time it rained, and their beards were bushy and unkempt.

Quint pulled the cigar from his mouth. "Like I said yesterday, one hundred dollars to each of you to lean hard on the people I tell you to."

"How do we lean on them?" the one in the miner's cap said.

"Any way I tell you to. The thing the boss wants is to strike fear into 'em. Scare 'em, and scare 'em good."

The other one nodded. "I think we can do that."

Then Quint noticed two riders approaching from further along Willbury Street, which was called Willbury Road until it reached town. They reined up in front of the marshal's office, and Quint squinted to see them. One was Johnny McCabe, and the other a blonde girl. Looked like the one he had seen the day before, when he had been watching the ranch.

"Well, son-of-a-gun. They're coming right to us."

The one with the miner's cap followed Quint's gaze. "That them?"

The other shook his head. "Now, hold on. That there's Johnny McCabe."

Miner's Cap looked at Quint. "That right? You're talking about us picking a fight with Johnny McCabe?"

Quint gave them both a long look. "You saying you boys are scared? I didn't take you for yella."

The one in buckskin shook his head. "Not yella. Just not suicidal."

They watched while the girl continued riding along, and McCabe swung out of the saddle in front of the marshal's office. Just beyond the marshal's office, a man approached, walking along and leading a horse, but otherwise the street was deserted.

"That girl," Quint said. "I want you to stay with her. Wherever she stops, I want you to put the fear of God in her."

Miner's Cap was watching her. "How?"

"Any way you like."

Buckskin shook his head. "Not for just a hundred dollars. That's Johnny McCabe's daughter."

Quint shook his head. "Two hundred each."

"Three."

Quint shrugged his shoulders. "The boss prob'ly won't mind, as long as you do your job. Do anything you want to her, but leave her alive so she can be real scared. So the family can be real scared."

Em said to Johnny, "I'll be down at the Second Chance, visiting with Aunt Ginny."

She rode along, enjoying the day. The mountain was clear and dry and the sun felt good on her shoulders.

She hopped down from her horse in front of the Second Chance and gave the rein a couple of turns around the hitching rail.

She turned to head up and onto the boardwalk, but she found two men standing in front of her. One in a miner's cap and the other in buckskin pants.

"Excuse me." She went to step around them, but they moved over to block her path.

"You're comin' with us, little lady." Miner's Cap was grinning.

The other said, "Where you wanna do this?"

"Right out behind the saloon would be good."

"Won't they hear her screamin'?"

Miner's Cap shook his head. "You do it right, you hurt her bad enough, there won't be any screamin'. I lived with the Apache when I was a kid. They could make a man die in the worst kind of misery, but with no screaming at all."

She took a step backward, but they moved with her and each grabbed her by an arm.

"Please. Don't hurt me."

As though they hadn't heard her at all, they marched her down along the side of the Second Chance and out behind it.

"Sorry to have to do this, little lady," Miner's Cap drew his knife. "But we're being paid mighty good to do this."

She backed away from him but bumped into

Buckskin who had stepped behind her. He grabbed her by the shoulders.

"How do you do this so she won't scream?"

Miner's Cap was grinning, like a cat that had caught a mouse. "Very first thing you do is cut her tongue out."

Em's eyes went wide as he stepped toward her.

A man spoke from behind him. "Let her go."

Em looked past him to see James Colter standing at the corner of the building.

Miner's Cap faced him. "Get out of here, cowboy. This don't concern you."

"If you mean to hurt the lady, then it does."

Buckskin pushed Em away, and then he and Miner's Cap went for their guns. Colter was faster, pulling his revolver and cocking it in one motion and firing from the hip. One bullet found the chest of Miner's Cap. The other went into Buckskin. Neither got off a shot.

Buckskin went down to his knees, blood already soaking into his shirt around a bullet hole. The other man stumbled about, like a drunk man trying to do some clogging, and he fell face forward to the ground.

The man in buckskin looked up at Colter in surprise, and then he toppled over.

Colter stood with his gun ready. "You all right, Miss McCabe?"

She was sitting up in the dirt. She nodded her head but couldn't find any words.

He walked over to the men and pulled the guns from their grip. "Just in case there's any life left in them. I doubt there is, but just in case. I've seen more than one man mortally wounded on the battlefield do a whole lot of killing before he breathed his last."

He tossed the guns aside and holstered his own revolver. Then he reached down to help Em to her feet.

Johnny and Tom came running around to the back of the saloon, their guns drawn.

Em said, "I'm all right, Pa. These two were going

to hurt me, but Mister Colter saved my life."

Then she looked at Colter and corrected herself. "*Reverend* Colter."

Tom said, "Reverend *James* Colter?"

Colter nodded.

"We've been expecting you. The Methodist Church let me know you were coming and asked me to watch for you. They said you might be coming by horseback."

Colter smiled. "They know me all too well."

20

THEY ALL SAT at a table in the Second Chance. Johnny had a cup of coffee in front of him, and so did Tom and Colter.

Aunt Ginny said, "This girl doesn't need coffee. She needs something else."

And Ginny fetched her a glass of white wine.

Hunter stood at the stove in the center of the room pouring himself a cup of coffee. "To think they were trying to do this right out back."

Em stared toward the table, saying nothing. She was clearly shaken. Ginny sat at the table with a cup of tea in front of her, and she reached over and placed a hand on Em's. "You're safe, now."

Em nodded.

"There are truly monsters in this world."

Em nodded again. "I just didn't expect them to be so close to home."

She looked at Johnny. "Are those the kind of men you dealt with, back in your years along the Mexican border?"

Johnny nodded. "Dealt with some in other places, too, including around here."

Tom took a sip of coffee. "I went through their pockets. Nothing at all to identify them."

Em said, "They told me they were hired and were paid really well."

Colter took a sip of coffee and set his cup back on the table. "I'm just glad I came along when I did."

He looked at Em. "I was leading my horse down the street when I saw them take you out behind the saloon."

"I'll always owe you."

He shook his head. "Nonsense. God put me in the right place for a reason. He protects His children."

Johnny looked at him. "We weren't very hospitable to you this morning. I owe you an apology."

Colter shook his head. "Not necessary. I suppose I do look like a saddle bum and a gunfighter."

Johnny looked at Tom. "Why is it all the Methodist ministers in my life look like gunfighters?"

Tom grinned.

Colter said, "I was in the Army for a few years. Cavalry. We fought the Apache down in New Mexico Territory and I saw my share of battle."

"Your share of battle." Johnny shook his head. "No one should ever have to experience battle."

"Agreed. After I was discharged, I just roamed for a while. Then I began reading a Bible. It had been in my saddlebags right along. My mother had given it to me when I joined the Army, but I never even opened it until a few years after I was discharged. I knew all the stories from when I was growing up. My mother was a God-fearing woman and she made sure my brothers and sisters and I all went to church. But when I started reading it myself, after two years of warfare, of seeing men on both sides die and even doing some killing myself, the stories took on a whole new meaning. Somehow, they weren't just stories anymore."

Tom looked at him. "And then you had the calling."

Colter nodded. "And then I got the calling. So I studied to join the ministry, and now here I am. I've served as an assistant pastor, but this will be my first time as the head pastor."

Em gave a little grin, despite all she had been through. "I'm sure you'll do fine."

He returned the grin, then he looked over at Tom. "So, what do we do about those men, Reverend McCabe?"

Tom chuckled. "It's just *Marshal,* now."

"The bishop still refers to you as *Reverend.*"

Tom shook his head with a grin. "God help him."

He took a sip of coffee. "We're going to deal with this by being more cautious, by going about as though we're expecting trouble. If those men were hired, then the one who hired them is still out there. Danny and I will be walking our rounds with shotguns in our hands even on weekdays and Sundays. And I plan to hire some more deputies until this is over." He looked at Johnny. "Want to wear a badge?"

"Not really, but I will. And I'll tell Dusty and Charles that one of them is to be at the ranch house at all times, unless I'm there."

He looked at Em. "And..."

She finished it for him. "I'm to stay close to the house. Believe me, you won't have to tell me twice."

Tom said, "I'll ride out and ask Father if he might wear a badge, too."

Ginny looked at Johnny. "Anyone in this town would have to be insane to cause trouble with both Johnny and Matt McCabe wearing badges."

"Do you think Sam will mind being deputized?"

Sam was in the valley, purchasing some chicken meat. They bought most of it from Carter Harding. "I'll send him over to your office once he's back."

Once the coffee was finished, the group dispersed. Johnny said to Ginny, "Do you mind if Em waits here with you? I have to run one more errand before I take her back to the ranch."

Ginny looked at Em with a smile. "She's welcome here anytime."

Hunter placed a scattergun across the bar. "She'll be safe here. I guarantee it."

Johnny nodded. "That's what I wanted to hear."

He headed out the door and across the street to the hotel.

On the front porch, he drew his revolver and checked the loads. On second thought, he thumbed a sixth cartridge into the cylinder and then slid the gun back into his holster, making certain it was a little loose should he have to grab it in a hurry.

He stepped in and found a man standing behind the front desk. He was about Johnny's height, with thinning hair parted in the middle, and he wore a jacket and a string tie.

Johnny didn't wait for the man to ask if he could help him. "I'm looking for the room of Hiram McCabe."

"Actually, he's in the lounge at the moment."

Without another word, Johnny strode through the doorway that opened to the lounge.

He never knew why it was called a lounge. It was really a small saloon. A bar filled the far side of the room, and tables were scattered between the door and the bar.

Hiram sat at one of the tables. A bottle stood on the table, and he held a glass in his hand. He looked at the doorway through a whiskey haze and saw Johnny, and he gave a slow, whiskey-addled blink of surprise.

Johnny strode toward the table. Without a word of greeting, he grabbed Hiram by the lapels of his jacket and pulled him out of the chair. The whiskey in the glass dumped over the front of his jacket, and his leg bumped the table and the bottle fell over.

"Two men almost killed one of my daughters today."

Hiram tried to find words but all that came out was a stammer.

Johnny said, "They were hired, and they said they were being paid a lot of money. That could point a finger right at you."

Hiram managed to get out the words, "Johnny, I assure you..."

"They're both dead. They were killed before they could hurt her. But if I ever find out it was you who hired them, I'll break your neck. You understand me?"

A man at another table got to his feet. He had a narrow build and white hair, but dark eyes like two lumps of coal in a snow drift. "Now, see here! Unhand that man or I'll call for the marshal."

Johnny ignored him and kept his gaze on Hiram. "Do you understand me? I don't care who you are or whose son you are, or how much money you have. If I ever find out you're responsible, I'll break your neck. Right here, in front of everyone."

The man standing said, "Threats like that can get you thrown in jail, you hooligan."

Johnny looked over at him. "There's no jail that can hold me."

Something in Johnny's voice, or the look in his eyes, made the man take a step back.

Johnny let Hiram go, and Hiram fell back to his chair.

"You threaten my family and there is no law. There's just you and me. You understand?"

Hiram nodded.

Johnny turned and strode out the door, the heels of his boots driving themselves into the floorboards and his spurs making a little music.

The white-haired man walked over to Hiram. "Are you all right, sir?"

Hiram nodded, straightening out his rumpled jacket. The toppled bottle on his table had created a stream of whiskey that fed a small puddle on the floor.

"I'm Judge Mather, newly appointed by Governor White. I am here for the trial of Judge Mack. Would you like to file charges against that man?"

Hiram shook his head. "I'll be fine. But thank you."

He had consumed a little too much whiskey, but being hauled out of your chair by Johnny McCabe and threatened to have your neck broken has a way of sobering a man up.

Hiram had no idea what Johnny had been talking about regarding a threat on his daughter, but Hiram thought quickly, and came up with an equation that would seem to explain what had happened.

He knew Quint liked a saloon on the far side of town. *The Gold Nugget.* Hiram grabbed his hat and headed out the door.

The Gold Nugget was on D Street, which intersected with Willbury a few blocks beyond the marshal's office. It would take Hiram a few minutes to get there, which was good. He could use the air.

The barroom was smaller than the Second Chance, and it was dimly lit. Tobacco smoke swirled about overhead, and the place smelled of smoke and stale beer. The floor near the bar was stained from tobacco juice that had missed the spittoons. Hiram found Quint at the bar.

Quint looked at him with an amused smile. "What brings you here?"

"Apparently two men tried to hurt one of Johnny McCabe's daughters."

Quint still had the grin. "That so?"

"I found out about it because he thinks I'm the one behind it and he threatened to break my neck."

Quint shrugged his shoulders. "All he did was threaten. Words won't hurt you none."

"The girl's fine, in case you want to know. Both men are dead."

Quint shrugged again. "That means we don't have to pay 'em. They weren't smart enough to ask for some of the money up front."

He reached for a glass of whiskey on the bar in front of him and downed it.

Hiram was staring at him. "You hired those men."

"Look, city boy. I'm here to do a job. I do the job I'm paid for."

"That finishes it. I'm done. I'm going to the marshal and I'm telling him everything."

Quint pulled a knife, so fast Hiram barely saw him move, and the tip of the blade was suddenly under Hiram's nose. He didn't dare flinch out of fear that it might cut him a third nostril.

"Now you listen here, city boy. You say a word and I'll gut you like a pig. You got that?"

"You'll hang."

"But you'll still be gutted like a pig. It won't kill you at once. You'll live a few minutes, bleeding to death, and it won't be pleasant. You'll be in more pain than you can imagine. You want to die that way?"

Hiram said nothing.

"Now you be a good boy and run back to the hotel and drink your whiskey."

Hiram turned and walked out to the street.

He was faced with one man who wanted to break his neck and another who wanted to gut him like a pig. Not that he knew how a pig was gutted, but it didn't sound good.

If he were a true McCabe, he thought, if he had the survival skills his brothers had and that McCabe men seemed to be somehow born with, he would saddle up and just ride. Head to Texas or some such place and live under an assumed name. But he didn't know enough about survival to make it through even one night in the wilderness. He was wise enough to admit that to himself.

He began walking back to the hotel.

21

JOHNNY AND MATT SAT on the front porch of the
ranch house, looking out at the darkness beyond.
Crickets chirped and a cool night breeze touched them.
As usual, when the brothers got together they pulled the
cap from a bottle of scotch, and they each sat with a
glass.

"I'm glad Em's all right." Matt sat in the rocker
that had originally been placed on the porch for Aunt
Ginny.

Johnny used a wooden upright chair he kept on
the porch. The chair was old and the finish long since
worn off, because it was out here regardless of the
weather. But it was still solid and served its purpose. "I
wouldn't say she's all right. She wasn't hurt physically,
but she's deep down scared."

Matt nodded. "You ever been scared like that?"

Johnny shook his head. "Can't say that I have.
Things scare me, sure, but I've never been scared like
that."

"Yeah. Maybe it's because we're fighters. We never
really feel disempowered."

Johnny grinned. "You look up those words just so
you can use 'em in conversation?"

Matt returned the grin. "No. I'm just that smart."

Johnny laughed. "I wish Joe was here. I really like
visiting with you, but somehow it never feels quite
complete unless Joe's here, too."

"I know how you feel. The three of us came west
together. You and Joe had already been West. You had
been as far as Texas and Joe as far as the Rockies. But
the three of us, we rode horseback all the way from
Pennsylvania to California. Learned a lot on the way."

"Pursuing a killer we never did catch. But I
wouldn't change any of it for the world. Except for the
part about Pa being shot."

"You ever think about that day? The day Pa was

killed?"

Johnny shrugged. "Sometimes. Not much, anymore. It used to haunt my dreams."

"Mine, too. But do you realize how long it's been?"

"Thirty-three years. Hard to believe. In a way, it seems like yesterday."

"I wonder if we would even recognize the killer if we should, say, pass him on the street in Jubilee."

Johnny shrugged. "Some men don't change much over the years, but some change a whole lot."

Matt took a belt of whiskey. "So, tomorrow we put on deputy badges and begin working as law enforcement officers."

Johnny nodded his head. "The trial starts day after tomorrow. Tom and Danny will be busy guarding the prisoner."

"I've got to wonder just what's going on. I have the gut feeling it's all somehow related. What happened to Em, the trial and Hiram being in town."

Johnny cocked his head a little in a sort of shrug. "Well, Hiram's one of the witnesses against Judge Mack."

"No, I mean more than that. Some sort of deeper connection."

Johnny took a gulp of whiskey and paused a moment while he enjoyed the taste. "I didn't mention this to the women, but I paid a little visit to Hiram this afternoon."

"Oh?"

"Something Em said, something those two men told her, before our new minister shot 'em down. They told her they were being paid well to hurt her."

"That would seem to imply that someone with money was behind it."

Johnny nodded. "And who do we know in town who has a lot of money?"

"Hiram."

"I've been having that same gut feeling you're having, that these things are somehow connected. So I paid him a visit. Of course, I did it my way."

Matt chuckled. "So, what happened?"

"I hauled him off of his chair by the front of his jacket and told him if I ever find out he was the one who hired those men, I would break his neck. And, wouldn't you know, the new judge happened to be sitting at one of the tables. I guess I made a good first impression on him."

Matt laughed. "I'm glad to see there is one thing in this world that hasn't changed."

"What's that?"

"You."

Johnny laughed.

"One thing though, Johnny. Hiram's my responsibility. I'm at least partly at fault for him being the way he is. If he has to be dealt with, I'll do it."

Johnny nodded.

Matt took another sip of whiskey and let his gaze drift out into the night.

Jack handed a cup of coffee through the bars to Judge Mack, then he pulled over a stool and sat.

The Judge sat on the edge of his bunk and took a sip of coffee. "The world is sure getting complicated, Jack. I miss the old days, when if a man was getting rough with a woman you just put a bullet in him and that was the end of it. Justice came from the business end of a gun."

Jack nodded. "You sound like my father."

"I think that's prob'ly a good thing."

The Judge looked at his cup. "You got something stronger?"

Jack grinned. "I thought you might want something, so I came prepared."

He reached into his jacket and pulled out a tin flask. The Judge tossed his coffee out the jail window to the alley outside, and then he held the cup out to Jack, through the bars. "Fill 'er up, barkeep."

Jack grinned and filled the cup to the halfway

point.

Mack took a sip. "Bourbon."

"Hope you don't mind. I prefer it to scotch."

"At this point, as long as it's wet and strong is all I care about."

Mack went back to the edge of his bunk. "If it weren't for Angie, I'd just bust out of here and you'd never see me again."

Jack grinned. "Judge, I shouldn't be hearing that."

Mack waved a hand to dismiss the notion. "You can't testify that you heard anything. Attorney-client privilege."

"I'll say one thing. You surely do know the law."

Mack nodded. "You ever hear my story?"

"Only how you became judge and jury on a posse down in Texas, a lot of years ago. It's how you got your name."

"I mean, how I come West. You ever hear the story of young Hannibal McIntyre?"

Jack shook his head, so the Judge told him of his early days.

1855

HE ATTENDED law school because his father wanted him to. The McIntyres came from a long line of lawyers and judges, going back to England prior to the Revolution. But Hannibal had no interest in the law. He attended law school for his father, and he did well because he wanted his father to be proud of him. But his passion was not something his father approved of.

His passion was boxing.

His name was Hannibal William McIntyre, Junior, and he was called Hannibal when he attended classes at Yale. But when he stepped into the ring, much to his father's dismay, he was Billy Mack.

He stood a little taller than average, with sandy hair, and a nose that was a bit crooked because it had been broken in the ring a year earlier. He had strong shoulders and bulging biceps, and a rippled stomach. He could punch hard and fast, and he had stamina. He was nearly as strong and fast in the late rounds of a fight as he was in the early ones.

In those days, you fought until one of the fighters went down, and Mack had never been the one who went down. By the time he was twenty-one years old, he had a law degree from Yale, which made his father proud, and he was 18-0 in the ring, which made Mack himself proud. He had even won the fight where his nose had gotten broken.

His father sent out query letters to law firms and one in Boston was willing to take him on. Mack's father said to him, "I'm sure it will be the start of a brilliant career in law."

Mack would have to quit boxing, of course. He agreed to do so, but he already had one more fight scheduled. There was too much money bet on the fight for him to pull out. But he told his father this would be his last.

His opponent, Jake Canner, was taller and stronger than Mack, but not as fast on his feet or with his fists. Gamblers had placed the odds on Mack, five to one.

Mack had been given an offer of two thousand dollars if he would throw the fight. Two thousand back then was more than most farmers made in a year, though pocket change to a McIntyre. Mack turned down the offer, but he would have done so even if his family had not been wealthy. This was to be his last fight, and he wanted to go out with honor.

One thing about Mack—he had an explosive temper. As the fight progressed, Canner clenched with him in a corner and tried to gouge an eye with his thumb. The ref didn't see it so no penalty was called, but Mack felt anger exploding inside him.

He backed Canner into a corner and drilled him with a hard left. Then a hard right. Canner blocked the first punch by raising a forearm, but the second one caught him squarely on a cheekbone and rocked his head back.

Mack didn't wait to see if the man was hurt, but came at him with another left. This one caught Canner at the right eyebrow and opened a gash. Then Mack cut loose with a drilling uppercut. He watched while his opponent's eyes rolled back and his knees buckled.

The ref stepped between Mack and the downed fighter. He looked at Mack. "Back to your corner."

Mack stood there, wanting the fighter to get up so Mack could drive another fist into him.

"Back to your corner!"

Mack's coach called to him from just beyond the ropes, in the corner designated as Mack's. The man was about forty, with red hair and a brown fedora, and an Irish accent. "Billy, me boy. Get back here."

Mack turned and walked back to his corner.

"Lemme see yer hand."

Fighting was bare-knuckle in those days, and one of his punches had opened a gash along his right middle knuckle. A little tendril of blood was working its way down along his finger.

"Here, lemme tape that up while we have time."

Mack looked back while his coach went to work on his hand. Canner was still down, not moving.

The ref counted to ten and then stood and raised his hands in the air and the bell was sounded, and the crowd of three hundred began cheering.

The ref pointed to Mack and called out, "The winner!"

With his right hand now taped enough that the flow of blood stopped, Mack walked toward the ref, and the ref grabbed Mack by the hand and raised his hand in the air, and the crowd cheered more.

Canner was still not moving.

Canner's coach knelt beside him and then looked up at the ref. "We need a doctor."

The ref called out, "Is there a doctor here?"

One man stepped from the crowed. Gray haired and in a suit and tie. He climbed into the ring and knelt beside Canner, and he checked for a pulse. He pulled back one of Canner's eyelids for a look at his eye.

"This man is dead."

The following day, Mack stood before a judge, his father at his side. The judge announced he would be remanded for trial, on the charge of second-degree murder. Mack was released into his father's custody for a bail of five thousand dollars.

That night, with a glass of sherry in one hand, Mack said to his father, "I can't believe they're charging me with murder. It was an accident."

Hannibal McIntyre, Senior, with gray mutton chops and wearing a satin smoking jacket over a white shirt and tie, looked at his son. "I spoke with the prosecuting attorney, off the record. Not the most ethical thing to do, but he and I have known each other since we were younger than you. We went to law school together. He was in the crowd at that boxing match, and he said you were vicious. Your eyes were like those of a wild animal smelling blood and going in for the kill."

"It wasn't like that, Father."

"Then, what was it like?"

Mack shrugged. "I was mad. Sure. The other fighter—he tried to gouge me in the eye. That's against the rules but the ref didn't see it. I got mad and started hitting him fast and hard."

"You must have hit him really hard. The man's neck was broken."

Mack shook his head. "I'm so sorry."

"I wanted you to give up that hooligan sport, but you refused. You said you wanted one more fight, and you got what you wanted. Not only might this end your law career before it can even get started, but it might end your freedom itself. Not to mention what it could do to *my* career."

His father went upstairs, leaving Mack standing

alone in the parlor. Mack looked into the fire as he finished his glass of sherry and poured another.

Despite his two glasses of sherry, when he went upstairs to bed he found he couldn't sleep. He might have drifted away a little, but for the most part, he stared at the ceiling.

He was still awake when the darkness outside his window faded into morning light. He remained with his head on the pillow as he heard his father's carriage outside, making its way along the cobblestone driveway and out to the street beyond.

A moment later, Herman poked his head into the doorway. Herman was a black man who served the family as butler. Since this was Massachusetts and there had been no slavery here since 1783, Herman's was a paid position.

"Mister Hannibal," he said. "Are you awake?"

"Afraid so."

"Mrs. McIntyre wants to see you in the kitchen right away."

Mack figured, *Why not?* His father had made it clear how ashamed he was of his only son. Now it could be Mother's turn. Mack got dressed and went downstairs.

He found his mother waiting for him by the kitchen table. She was in a lacy housecoat, and an equally lacy night cap was pulled down over her hair and tied under the chin. She generally didn't come downstairs until fully dressed, so Mack was a little surprised.

"You have my temper," she said, without even a *good morning* as a preamble.

"So it would seem."

"I can't let my only son hang or go to prison."

Mack didn't quite know what to say, so he said, "I'm not in favor of it, either."

"Your father has headed into the city to his office. He won't be home until six o'clock tonight. You can have a ten hour head start before he even knows you're gone."

Mack didn't know if he had heard her right. "Head start?"

"You will have to run, my son."

"Run? To where? Canada?"

She shook her head. "West. They will never find you there."

Herman materialized at his side. Mack never knew how a man in hard leather shoes could move so silently, but Herman often did.

"I have a horse saddled for you, Mister Hannibal. A few days' worth of provisions in the saddlebags. And this."

He handed Mack a revolver. Mack had hunted fox with his father and shot skeet, but he had never fired a revolver.

Herman said, "It's a Colt Navy. Thirty-six caliber. I'll show you how to load it."

And he did, using the kitchen table, with Mother watching.

Herman said, "I have reloading supplies in your saddlebags. Balls, gunpowder, patches, a tin of percussion caps."

Herman handed the gun back to Mack. "You don't aim it like a rifle. You just point, like you were pointing with your finger, and you shoot."

Mother said, "And now you must ride."

"For how long?"

She shrugged her shoulders and shook her head. Tears were rolling their way down her cheeks. "For as long as is necessary."

People in the McIntyre family didn't hug each other. Men would shake hands. A man would gently grasp a woman's hand and bring it to his lips for a light kiss. But they never embraced.

But Mack figured, *Why not?* He might never see his mother again, so he pulled her in for a hug. Then he shook Herman's hand.

And then he ran.

Outside, he swung into the saddle and took one more look at the only home he had ever known. Virtually a palace, with tall white pillars holding up a roof two floors above. Vines crawled up the front wall.

Then he turned and rode away.

He took his mother's advice and headed West. He stopped shaving, so he wouldn't be easily recognizable. And he started calling himself by his boxing name, Billy Mack.

Once he was west of the Missouri, he turned south to Texas and learned how to tend cattle. Or *punch cows*, as the cowhands said. He let his hair grow, and he stopped speaking with the erudite version of English he had learned.

He drank whiskey with the boys and smoked hand-rolled cigarettes. One year blended into another and his hair reached his shoulders, and his skin grew rough from exposure to the sun and wind.

He was often restless, so he would stay with one cattle outfit for a few months and then ride on. He took other jobs, too, whatever might be available in whichever area he landed in. Serving beer, riding shotgun for a stagecoach company, deputy marshal.

He began wearing his gun like he knew how to use it. Not belt-high but a little lower at his right hip, so he could get to it in a hurry. And then he started wearing a second gun so he could get more shots off before he had to reload.

Mack now spoke with a whiskey-soaked voice, and his speech was filled with words like *ain't*. His Yale education now seemed useless to him. He felt his real education had begun the moment he crossed the Missouri.

He eventually took a job as deputy marshal in Wardtown, working for Marshal Mose Watkins, and where he eventually got the name *Judge*.

*   *   *

Jack asked, "Did you ever hear from your mother

or father again?"

Mack shook his head. "We were never close. They were always stern. Distant. The only kind thing my mother did for me was telling me to ride away. I never knew what love was until I met Angie. I've known women over the years, but something about her makes something come alive inside me."

"If you don't mind my asking, why haven't you married her by now?"

Mack shrugged. "I guess maybe I was afraid of re-creating what my parents had. They were distant from each other. Sat at opposite ends of the table. Had separate bedrooms. She had her sitting room and he had his smoking room. Away from the dinner table, I don't remember them ever saying a word to each other. It's no wonder I had no brothers or sisters."

Jack noticed the Judge's harsh, mountain man way of speaking seemed to be falling away.

Mack said, "I suppose all the years on the trail, I was just running from the dispassionate life I was raised to. Maybe I went too far a few times."

He took another sip of whiskey. "Angie is a girl my mother and father would have disapproved of severely. Hardly any education at all. She can barely read. Not refined in the least. But you know what I like about her? She's real. She doesn't put on airs for anyone. And she has such an incredible heart."

"Judge, you're not your parents. Looks to me like you left that life behind long ago. Looks like you might have been leaving it behind even before you rode out, pursuing boxing the way you did. Your father disapproved of it, but it was your passion regardless."

The Judge shrugged his shoulders.

"Marry her, Judge. That's what I say. When this trial is over, marry her and build a life with her."

"I killed him, you know. That man. Harold Higgins, they say his name is. I shot him down. That's the real reason I didn't want you defending me. You McCabes—you're good people. Noble. Like something out of those old stories of knights and villains and such. Like King Arthur and his ilk. I didn't want you compromising yourself."

"How would I be doing that? The two witnesses can't agree on their stories. That brings their credibility into question. It's the word of two questionable witnesses against yours. Guilt can't be proven beyond a reasonable doubt."

Mack shook his head. "I did it, Jack. I shot him down. When I came across him attacking Angie, I fully intended to kill him. I didn't want Angie to have to see it, so I got him out of the room and threw him down the stairs. When he got to his feet, I came downstairs to finish the job. I'm still a fair hand at fighting with my fists and I intended to beat him to death, but when he grabbed Miss Maybelle's gun I decided to end it that way. But I fully intended to kill him. There was no self-defense about it."

Jack shrugged his shoulders. "In your place, if it had been Nina being attacked, I would have done the same thing."

"Even so, I don't want you compromising yourself in court, defending a man you know is guilty."

"There's a thing about my family that's a little hard to understand at first."

The Judge was listening.

"We believe in justice, but not a justice that's defined by legislation and interpreted by the courts. We believe in a simpler justice. A truer one. A larger one. Often, a court of law is about which side has the better lawyer, not about what's right and wrong. But my family defends the right from the wrong. Even if it had been me who found that Higgins man attacking Miss Angie, or any woman, I would have killed him. So would Pa have, and Dusty and Josh. And my uncles, Matt and Joe. Because that's who we are."

Mack nodded his head, letting all Jack had said settle on him. "What makes you all like that? Where's it come from?"

Jack shrugged. "Seems to be a family tradition. Pa says his father was like that, and his grandfather. The first John McCabe, my father's great grandfather, was like that. He was a contemporary of Daniel Boone. Fought in the Revolution, and he explored the mountains of Pennsylvania and Virginia, when it was all still a frontier. He had those values of justice. He claimed it came from his father."

"You know, I've heard the name John McCabe before, when I was growing up back East. I had forgotten. His name was still known."

"I can't let you hang, Judge. Not for the same kind of thing I would have done, or any of the men in my family would have done." Jack shook his head with a chuckle. "If Bree had caught him, she would have thrown him out a window and then shot him for good measure."

"What about Hiram McCabe? The son of your Uncle Matt?"

"I'm not sure what to think about him. Tom and Danny's brother. It's said he's not really a McCabe, that Matt isn't his real father. But it doesn't matter. Even if Matt really is his father, Hiram is no McCabe. Being a part of this family isn't really about blood relation."

Mack was silent a moment, staring down at the floor. Then he drew a breath. "Jack, I wish there were more families like yours. The world would be a better place."

22

JOHNNY STEPPED into the kitchen before the sun had even begun to peek over the horizon. The room was dark and Johnny brought a lantern to life and stood it on the table. Then he began to build a fire in the stove.

He figured Jessica worked hard enough, so he made certain he was awake before her every morning to get the fire going and make the first pot of coffee. He had done the same for Lura, years ago.

He worked the hand pump in the kitchen and filled the coffee kettle and then reached for a canister of coffee that Jessica kept on the counter.

When the coffee was nearly ready, he heard a rider out back. He figured who it was, so he didn't bother to investigate.

The back door opened and Dusty stepped in. "Coffee smells good, Pa. Looks like my timing is right."

As Johnny poured Dusty a cup, Charles and Bree arrived.

Johnny said to them, "This will be my first day working as a deputy in town for Tom. I'll probably be needed at least until the trial is finished. Are you sure you can handle things here?"

Bree nodded. "Don't worry, Pa. I'll keep 'em in line."

"And remember," he looked from Dusty to Charles, "I want one of you here at the house at all times."

They both nodded their heads.

Johnny held a cup of coffee and he looked at Dusty. "In fact, it might be safer if you and Haley and Jonathan move in here until we know what's going on, considering what almost happened to Em." He glanced over to Bree. "You two, as well."

Dusty stood with his coffee in one hand. "What do you think it is, Pa? What's going on with all of this?"

Bree said, "This is a rough country and

sometimes bad things happen. But my gut feeling is what happened to Em and the man who was watching the house are both somehow related."

Charles nodded. "And whoever cut the wire. There's no obvious reason for anyone doing that, and it sure didn't happen by accident."

Johnny took a sip of coffee. "Always listen to your gut. It's the one part of you that can't be fooled. I got that piece of advice from three different men over the years. My own father said it more than once when I was growing up. Then the Cheyenne shaman Many Lives told me that, and then I heard it from Mister Chen."

Bree nodded. "Mister Chen said that to me a couple of times, too."

"And my gut feeling is every bit of this is somehow tied into the trial of Judge Mack. I haven't been able to put it all together yet, but until we figure it out we have to be extra careful. That's why I want everyone to move in here for a while. This place is well fortified, and it'll be easier to keep everyone safe if we're under one roof."

Dusty looked at Pa. "None of this started happening until Hiram showed up in town, and he's involved in the trial. It can't be coincidence."

"Something else those three taught me. There's no such thing as coincidence."

Quint stepped into Hiram's room. Hiram had begun leaving the door unlocked, otherwise Quint would bang on the door with his fist until he opened up. No need to annoy anyone else on the floor.

Quint had a rifle in one hand. Not a Winchester, like most men of the West seemed to carry these days. This one looked to be a single-shot.

Quint had a big smile. "What do you think of this?"

Hiram was fixing his tie and was about to go downstairs for morning coffee. "Looks like an old rifle."

"This here's a Springfield. It's ten years old but it ain't been shot much. Black powder can corrode a steel barrel somethin' fierce. I got it in a poker game last night."

Hiram rolled his eyes. "And what, pray tell, are you going to do with it?"

"Gonna do what I'm being paid for. Create all sorts of mayhem for the McCabes. The trial starts tomorrow, so we got today free. I'm riding into the valley with this rifle. Today, one of the McCabes dies."

Hiram turned to face him. "Don't tell me you're serious."

"I'm gonna shoot one of 'em with this here rifle. From a distance. Ain't gonna face 'em in a gunfight. That would be dumb."

Quint held the rifle out. "See this here thing on top? It's called a trapdoor lock. You flip it open and slide in a cartridge, then close it up and the gun's ready to fire. It's one of the best guns for shooting long distance."

"Thank you so much. Now I feel truly educated." Quint turned back toward the mirror and continued adjusting his tie.

"You know what your trouble is? Your attitude."

Hiram shook his head. "I'm going downstairs for coffee."

"Yeah, you do that, little man. You just make sure you say what you're supposed to say on the stand tomorrow."

"We won't be on the stand tomorrow, most likely. They will have to begin jury selection and that could take days."

"Well, whenever it is, you say what you're supposed to. Remember what'll happen if you don't. And don't even think about going to the town marshal to warn the McCabes about what I'm about to do. You won't live through the night if you do."

Dusty was two miles from the house, riding alongside the fence, when he found another section that had been cut. Three strands of barbed wire, all neatly severed at the same point.

He swung out of the saddle to have a closer look at the wire. The ends of the severed pieces were sharp, like they were when freshly cut.

Beneath his feet was sod, which didn't hold a track like fresh dirt would, but he saw some sections that were pushed down, like where a man had stood while he cut the fence.

This wasn't cut long ago, he thought. Maybe within the hour.

In his saddle was a carbine he had brought along from the ranch house. He wouldn't normally have brought along a rifle for ranch work, but these days he thought it wise.

He mounted up and pulled the rifle from the scabbard. It was a Winchester. He preferred a rifle he had acquired a few years ago, a Mauser .43 caliber. But the Mauser was back at the house he and Haley shared. He had grabbed the Winchester from the rifle rack at the main ranch house.

He saw no more sections of matted down grass, but he knew the man must have had a horse nearby. "Come on, boy," he said to his horse. "Let's go cut for sign."

He felt the impact of the bullet before he heard the *boom* of the gun. It hit him in the back and he felt his right arm go numb. The Winchester fell from his grip and flipped over the saddle horn and fell to the grass.

Dusty found he couldn't catch his breath. His first instinct was to dive from the saddle before another shot could be fired but he found he couldn't move.

Then blackness descended on him, like a curtain. He slumped over and fell from the saddle, landing in the grass beside his rifle.

Johnny finished walking his rounds and headed for the marshal's office. He hoped a pot of coffee was ready and waiting for him. As he finished his rounds, Matt would begin walking a new cycle. Tom's plan was to always have a law officer in motion about the town.

Felt strange having a badge pinned to his shirt. Johnny had been wanted by the law more than once, in his younger years. Now he was on the other side of the badge.

In Tom's office, he was greeted by the smell of fresh coffee. Just what he had hoped for.

Danny sat behind the desk with a cup and said, "Tom's gone over to Jack's office to talk about tomorrow's trial."

Johnny was about to reach for a coffee cup when he heard a commotion outside. A woman's voice calling out. "Pa! Jack!"

It was Bree. Johnny rushed out onto the boardwalk to see her on a horse charging down Willbury Street. Her hat was gone.

She brought her horse to a hard stop in front of Tom's office. The horse was lathered from the run—she must have pushed the horse hard all the way from the ranch. His hooves slid in the dirt as the horse came to a full, sudden stop.

"Pa, Dusty's been shot. Haley sent me to get Jack."

Doc Martin's office was across the street, on the second floor. He came hurrying over, buttoning his jacket. "I can come, young lady."

"Haley said to fetch Jack."

Danny stepped out behind Johnny. "He's at the office with Tom. I'll go fetch him."

And Danny took off running.

Johnny and Jack rode hard, the hooves of their horses clattering over the wooden bridge. Charles was waiting for them on the front porch when they reined up. "Where's Bree?"

"In town." Johnny swung out of the saddle. "Her horse was nearly done. She'll be along shortly."

Jack ran up the porch steps with Johnny following.

Charles said, "I'll take care of the horses."

Johnny and Jack found Dusty in the master bedroom. His shirt was off and he was lying face down on the bed. Haley had a towel over the wound and she was pressing down on it, trying to slow the flow of blood.

Jessica and Em were with her, ready to assist if necessary. But the only assistance they could provide was to hand Haley a fresh towel when the one she was using became too soaked with blood.

Jack held his medical bag in one hand. "I figured it was bad or you wouldn't have sent for me."

Haley looked up at him. "It was a large caliber. Tore into him and I think it might have broken a bone. I saw a few bone fragments in the wound. But surgery wasn't part of Granny Tate's teaching."

Johnny said, "It's been a long time since you did any doctoring, son. Can you do this?"

Jack nodded. "With a memory like mine, yes."

Johnny knew Jack wasn't bragging. He had seen Jack recite a page from a book he had read years earlier.

Haley stepped aside and Jack took a look. He lifted the towel and poked around the wound with a long, thin probe from his medical bag.

Haley said, "He's lost a lot of blood. We don't know how long he was lying out there before Charles found him."

Jack stood so he could face both Pa and Haley. "That bullet has to come out. Looks like it's fragmented so I'll be removing at least two pieces. Also looks like the bullet chipped his shoulder blade, so I'll be removing those bone fragments as well."

Haley nodded. "I'll assist."

Jack shook his head. "I fully respect your medical knowledge, more than most doctors I have met. But this is your husband."

Johnny said, "Jack's right. Is Jonathan here?"

She nodded. "Downstairs with Cora."

"You need to be downstairs with him."

Jack looked at Jessica. "Can you assist?"

"I've done midwife work for years."

"Good." To Haley: "Go downstairs. Wait with Jonathan."

Haley turned slowly. Reluctantly. She left the room and Em went with her.

Johnny looked to Jack. "I'll be with her. If you need anything, let me know."

Hiram didn't feel truly welcome at the Cattleman's Club, but he had to eat somewhere and he wasn't going to try the Second Chance. He decided the place where he would be the least reviled was the Cattleman's, so he took a table there.

The tall, dark woman who was working here came over. "So, you here to see if you can accuse anyone else of murder?"

He looked up at her, too tired to be angry. "I'm not accusing him of anything. I'm just providing testimony as to what I saw."

"The man who was killed was hurting Angie, and Angie is considered family here. Judge Mack saved her, and you're testifying against him. I don't know that I could say you're welcome here."

He nodded wearily. "I'm not welcome anywhere. But a man has to eat."

He reached into his jacket and pulled out his wallet and he laid two twenty dollar bills on the table, for a meal that he didn't think would cost more than two or three. "I'm simply hungry. The rest of that can be your tip."

The woman Hiram had heard called Miss Alisha walked up. "This man harassing you, Maybelle?"

Maybelle shook her head. "No. He's just trying to buy his way into being welcome so he can have a meal."

"That money looks about right, I suppose. What'll you have, Mister McCabe? And make it quick, because I want you out of here before the evening crowd starts coming in."

Maybelle said, "Of course, if anyone should be

shot and we need an expert witness, we know who to call."

Hiram ordered a steak with baked potatoes. "This is the most expensive steak I ever ordered. I hope it's good."

Maybelle grabbed the twenties. "You're lucky we're serving you at all."

It was after the steak was served that Quint came into the room. He made an entrance that caused two other diners in the room to turn and stare. His boots and hat were dusty and the front of his shirt was dark with sweat.

He pulled out a chair at Hiram's table and dropped onto it.

Mother had told Hiram once that you can often tell a lot about a man by the way he takes a chair. Some will lower themselves onto a chair with refinement and grace. That was how Hiram had learned to do it. Others would simply drop into a chair as though they were taking it by force. That's how Quint did it.

"Feel free to join me," Hiram said with sarcasm.

"Don't mind if I do."

Hiram didn't know if Quint caught the sarcasm and didn't care or was just being ignorant.

A goblet of wine stood beside Hiram's plate. Quint eyed it. "What's that?"

"A glass of wine I managed to coax from Miss Alisha."

Without asking, Quint reached across and grabbed it and took a belt. He grimaced and gave the glass back to Hiram. "That's awful."

"What do you expect for only forty dollars?"

Quint's mouth fell open. "You paid forty dollars for this? It tastes like vinegar and day-old socks."

"It's the special discount they offer for people they hate."

Hiram slid the glass aside. He wasn't going to drink after Quint. "What is it that brings you here?"

"I done me some shootin' today, with that new

164

rifle."

Hiram rolled his eyes. "How wonderful."

"Now we got us one less McCabe in the world."

Hiram looked at him. "Don't tell me you shot one of them."

Quint nodded, with a big smile. "Sure did. Right square in the back."

Hiram glanced about them. "Could you say it a little louder? I don't think they heard you out in the kitchen."

Quint lowered his voice. "It's what Mister Randall is paying me for."

"Which one did you shoot?"

Not Father, Hiram hoped. Please not Father.

Quint shrugged. "Don't know. One of the men. Don't really matter which one, does it? I waited at a distance and then plugged him right square in the back. That new rifle sure does shoot true."

Hiram shook his head. "You know if they manage to trail you back here, we're both dead men. You know that, don't you?"

"Don't worry yourself. You're like an old woman, you know that? They ain't gonna trace it to us. I covered my tracks real good."

He reached toward Hiram's plate. "You ain't gonna eat the rest of that steak, are you?"

Bree sat at the table. Cora puttered about the kitchen, wiping down a counter she had wiped down twice already. Johnny was on his feet, sometimes pacing a bit and other times standing still. He gripped a cup of coffee.

Em and Haley sat at the table across from Bree. They stared into nothingness and waited for word from upstairs.

Jonathan was eleven years old and stood nearly to Johnny's shoulder. He had dark hair and a lean build, and he wore a flannel shirt and jeans and riding boots. He was trying to be strong, to be a man like every other eleven year old boy Johnny had ever seen. But the only father he had ever known was upstairs with a bullet in him and maybe dying.

Johnny strolled over to the back door and looked out the window. Charles had gone out to tend to some of the wrangler duties, to keep himself busy while Bree waited with Haley. But Johnny saw Charles was just standing by the fence, leaning with his arms folded across the top rail.

Johnny figured he would go out and talk with him a bit. Stretch his legs and maybe take a break from pacing about the kitchen.

He didn't bother to fetch his hat, which was hanging on a peg on the parlor wall. He stepped out and Jonathan came with him.

"Figured I'd join you, sir, if you don't mind."

Johnny shook his head. "Don't mind at all."

A boy learns to be a man by watching other men.

As Johnny and Jonathan walked out toward the corral, Johnny saw a buckboard coming up the trail. He heard the clatter of hooves and the iron tires on the wagon wheels as it crossed the wooden bridge.

Jonathan said, "Looks like Mister and Mrs. Harding. Looks like they got Aunt Nina with them."

They pulled up and Charles came walking over.

Most people knew the man by the name Carter Harding, but at one time he had been an outlaw going by his given name, Harlan Carter. He was the tallest man Johnny had ever seen.

"I was in town." Carter spoke in a stiff-lipped, no-nonsense way. "Heard 'bout Dusty bein' shot and Jack was out here workin' on him. Fetched Nina and got the Mrs. And here we are."

Johnny nodded his head. "Mighty good to see you. Let's head into the kitchen and I can get you all some coffee."

Nina looked at him. "Any word yet on Dusty?"

Johnny shook his head. "Jack's still working on him."

Carter nodded. "Dusty's in good hands."

Charles said, "You folks go in with Pa. I'll take care of your rig."

Jonathan piped up. "Grampa. Another wagon's comin'."

Carter stood beside Johnny. "Looks like Doc Martin."

Johnny squinted toward the trail. "Your eyes are better'n mine."

Doc Martin drove a buggy pulled by one horse. He crossed over the bridge and pulled up beside the buckboard. "With Dusty shot, I should be the one tending him. I'm the doctor in town. You can't trust his life to a folk doctor and a former medical student."

Johnny said, "With all due respect, Doc, you're a country doctor. Jack was one of the best surgical students at Harvard. You're more than welcome to come in with us and we'll let Jack know you're here. But I don't think you should go up there unless he calls for you."

Harlan Carter said, "Jack knows what he's doing. Saved my leg a few years back when I took a bullet."

The crowd was too large for the kitchen and spilled over into the parlor. Doc Martin sat on the sofa looking like he felt out of place waiting while someone else was doing the doctoring.

Jonathan stood beside Johnny. "Grampa, someone has to let Uncle Josh and Aunt Temperance know."

Johnny nodded his head. "Once we get word on your Pa, I'll ride into town and send a telegram down to Medicine Bow."

Johnny stepped out onto the porch. Jonathan stepped out with him, and Johnny said, "How about you go into the kitchen and check on your Ma."

"Yes, sir."

Not that Johnny didn't want his grandson with him. It was just that he needed a moment alone, away from the crowd, to breathe the mountain air and maybe offer a little prayer for Dusty.

The coffee was still in Johnny's hand. He gave it a sip and found it had long since gone cold, so he let it fly over the rail.

Charles came walking up. "Got both rigs taken care of.

Johnny nodded. Then a question occurred to him. "Charles, you were the one to find him."

Charles nodded his head. "Dusty's horse came in without him. Bree was gonna ride out but I told her not to. I know you said you wanted either Dusty or me here at the house at all times, but I didn't want her out there alone."

"You did right."

"I told her to wait upstairs in a front window with a rifle and pick off any rider she didn't recognize."

Johnny couldn't help but grin at the thought of her up there with a rifle. "No one I'd rather have standing guard than Bree."

He set his empty cup on the porch rail. "Charles, tell me about what you found. All the details."

Charles stood beside him. The second tallest man Johnny had ever met. Charles leaned with one hand against a post that held up the porch roof. "Well, I back-trailed his horse. Found where the fence had been cut again, about two miles from the house. And that's where I found Dusty, face down in the grass. A bullet hole in the back of his right shoulder. I knew he was still alive because the back of his shirt was all wet with blood.

Johnny nodded. 'Dead men don't bleed."

"Pulled up a chunk of sod and used the mass of roots to plug the bullet hole as best I could. I was surprised he hadn't bled out already, because he must have laid there more'n an hour before I found him. When I got him back, Haley said bullet wounds are unpredictable. Sometimes the bullet itself will block some of the bleeding."

Johnny nodded. "I've seen it. Doesn't happen very

often but it does happen."

"I looked around real quick to see if I could see any sign of a rider, but I couldn't. And there was no time to look for one. I had to get Dusty back here to the house."

Johnny placed a hand on Charles' shoulder. "You did right."

Jonathan came running out. "Grampa! Come quick!"

Johnny found Jessica had come downstairs. Haley stood in front of her, too afraid to breathe.

Jessica said, "We got the bullet out. It had split into three fragments, and Jack got all three of them. Dusty's lost a lot of blood, but Jack thinks he'll be all right, in time."

Haley covered her mouth with both hands and tears began to flow. Jessica pulled her in for a hug.

Harlan Carter nodded his head in his stoic way. "Knew it. Jack knows what he's doin'."

Doc Martin was on his feet. "Sometimes digging for a bullet can cause a lot of tissue damage."

Jessica shook her head. "Not with Jack. He probed with such gentleness. That's what took so long."

Johnny nodded. "What about infection? Did he bathe the wound in corn liquor?"

Jessica grinned. "No, silly. He packed it with honey before he began sewing up the wound."

"Honey?"

Haley nodded, wiping away her tears. "Honey's one of the best things for preventing infection. Granny Tate showed me that and I told Jack about it."

Johnny said, "You mean I've been pouring corn liquor into my wounds all these years, but honey works as good?"

Haley nodded. "Better. Alcohol prevents infection to a large degree but it can also damage body tissue. Honey somehow works with the body to help the body fight infection while it mends."

"You don't say."

Haley and Nina headed upstairs to check on Dusty and Jack.

Johnny looked at his grandson. "Jonathan, we've got to postpone our ride into town. I'll send that telegram tomorrow and you can come with me. But right now, I have something to tend to."

Johnny gave Jessica a hug. Her neck was wet with sweat but she didn't smell bad. Somehow, this woman never smelled bad. He said, "Are you all right? You were up there a long time."

She nodded with a sigh. "I'm fine, but it has been a long day. I think I'm going to let Em and Cora fix supper tonight."

"Could you have them fix enough for everyone? We have a houseful and might as well invite them all."

She nodded.

Johnny said to Carter, "I'd take it as a favor if you and your wife would stay for supper tonight. I need you on hand. I have an errand to run and I figure Charles will want to come with me."

"You gotta go kill a man."

Johnny nodded. "But I don't want the house left unguarded. Bree is here, but I'd appreciate if you were here, too."

"Take your time and find the man. I'll be here when you get back."

"You see anyone approaching the house that you don't know, put a bullet in him."

"Won't be a problem."

23

"THIS IS WHERE I FOUND him." Charles sat in the saddle looking down at the three cut strands of barbed wire. He and Johnny had seen some steers grazing outside the pasture on the ride out from the ranch house, and one was standing a few yards from the fence opening, eyeing them warily. "With the cut in the fence, cows have been getting loose all afternoon."

"We'll round 'em up later, after we've dealt with more pressing matters." Johnny looked down at a small section of grass that was still matted down, where he figured Dusty must have fallen.

"We're just about where Dusty must have been shot." Charles glanced about. "If the shooter is still out there, then we're making targets out of ourselves."

"He better be a dang good shot, then, because there are two of us."

Johnny glanced toward the west. The sun was hanging near the horizon. "We've only got a couple of hours of sunlight left. Let's cut for sign. See if we can figure which direction he came from or rode off to."

Johnny rode off searching in one direction and Charles in the other. Didn't take Johnny long to find the place where the shooter had stood. He called out, "Over here!"

Charles rode over. A small pine stood five hundred feet from the fence, and the man had positioned himself behind it. Two cigarette stubs were in place.

Charles shook his head. "Not too smart. Could have started a grass fire."

"Smart enough to know how to do what he did, though. He cut the fence then just stood here and waited. Might have been here for hours."

They found where he had staked out his horse, about a hundred feet behind him. The grass matted down by the horse was only now starting to spring up.

Johnny said, "He knew not to keep his horse close. If you're lying in wait for a man, a horse can sometimes give you away."

"Think he had military training?"

Johnny rubbed his chin. "Maybe. Or he's ridden with raiders."

Charles glanced toward the western horizon. "We'd better get to trailing him. We're gonna run out of time soon."

"We won't find him today, but at least we'll know what general direction he rode off in."

They followed him across acres of sod. Most of the grass that had been pressed down as the horse stepped along had sprung back up, but the hoof prints in the ground itself were still visible if you looked close enough.

Johnny looked at Charles. "Let's ride single file. Stay back about fifteen or twenty feet. Just in case he's watching his back trail and wants to take a shot at us."

Johnny had a Winchester carbine in his saddle, and he pulled it free and rode with it across the front of his saddle. Charles did the same.

The trail they followed headed directly north. Within half a mile, they came to a stream that was six feet across and a foot deep. It cut across the valley and would eventually join with the small river near the ranch house. The river the bridge was built over.

The rider's tracks led into the stream but there were no tracks on the other side, meaning the rider rode in the stream for a while. The streambed was sandy in most places, and any tracks would have been washed away by the current long before now.

Charles rode up beside Johnny. "There's no way to know how far he rode before he turned out of the stream. Or which direction he rode in."

"We would have to ride in one direction and then if we didn't find where he turned out, ride in the other." Johnny glanced toward the west. The sun was touching the horizon. "But we're out of time."

"We can start again tomorrow at sunrise."

Johnny shook his head. "Tom will need me in town. The trial starts tomorrow."

Charles looked at him. "So he's gonna get away."

Johnny let out a long sigh, his thoughts drifting back to long ago and the man who shot his father. "Sometimes they do."

Jack was so exhausted that his joints hurt. He wanted nothing more than to climb into bed and sleep for half a day. Three hours of surgery, something he had never expected to do again. Added to the intensity was the fact that he had been operating on his brother. Digging through an open wound to search for fragments of a bullet, and bone fragments as well. Trying to find them all before Dusty lost too much blood.

And now Jack had to focus his exhausted mind on tomorrow's trial.

He knew he was too worn out to do it alone. So he climbed a set of wooden stairs that struck him as unnecessarily long.

The time was nine o'clock and the street was dark. Jack had taken Nina home before he came here, and as soon as this visit was over, he would be heading home and to that warm bed that waited for him.

From the street below he had seen a light was still on in a window of this second floor apartment. He knocked on the door and waited a moment, and then the door opened.

Origen Scott stood there, in a white shirt but with his tie long gone, and suspenders over his shoulders.

"Jack McCabe?"

"Sorry to bother you at this hour, Orrie. I have something I need to ask you."

Orrie rubbed his hands through his hair sleepily. Looked like he was ready for a warm bed, too. "Come on in."

He stepped aside and Jack moved past him and into the small apartment.

Jack found himself standing in the kitchen. Cupboards were against one wall, a cast iron stove against another, and in the corner of the room was a table. There was little room to maneuver around the table.

Orrie was young, not too long removed from law school, and was trying to run his new law practice on a shoe-string budget.

Jack said, "I just have something I want to ask you. The trial starts tomorrow, and I've just spent a good part of the day taking care of my brother Dusty, including three hours of surgery."

Orrie nodded his head. "I heard he was shot. News travels fast. Is he going to be all right?"

Jack nodded. "I think so. I got the bullet out, and now he just has to rest. Get his strength back. He lost a lot of blood but he's young and strong."

Orrie blinked with surprise. "You mean you did the surgery yourself?"

"Yeah. It's been quite a day. Dusty's wife Haley will supervise his recovery. She's a folk doctor, one of the best I've ever seen. Learned a lot from Granny Tate."

"I've heard the name Granny Tate. I guess she was around before I came to town. I also heard you were a medical student at one time but I didn't know you could do surgery. Is there anything you McCabes can't do? I half expect you to walk on water."

Orrie sounded a little bitter.

"Look, Orrie, I'm sorry about the way I took over the case. But I've come here to ask your help. I want you back on the case, working with me."

Orrie gave a weary sigh and his shoulders sagged. "Jack, I hate to admit it, but you were right to replace me. I was in over my head. I've only been out of law school fourteen months and I've never worked a murder trial before. I would have gotten Judge Mack hanged. I can't imagine what help I could possibly offer you."

"I need help with the leg work. Starting tomorrow morning, I need you to meet with the Judge. Mack, that is. Make sure he knows that tomorrow and likely the next few days will be about jury selection, but I want him to say nothing that Springer could use against him. I essentially want Mack to keep his mouth shut. I'm sure he understands about jury selection, but it's one thing to preside over a trial and another to be the defendant. And tell Miss Angie that she can't sit with him, even though she'll probably want to. She'll have to sit in the audience, maybe with Aunt Ginny."

Orrie nodded. "All right. I can do that. But where will you be?"

"I'm going to press for a mistrial first thing tomorrow, because Springer doesn't have a case. He might think he does, but he doesn't. I'll have the transcripts in hand that Myrna took during the Town Council meeting and I'll press to have them admitted as evidence. I have to go over the argument in my mind, anticipate any possible objections Springer might have. But to do that, I have to have a night's sleep first."

"Yeah, I can see you're about dead on your feet."

"I'll meet you at the Second Chance. I'll be there before the trial begins."

Orrie nodded. "All right, I'll do it. What about payment?"

"I'll pay you the same as I'm being paid."

"How much is that?"

Jack grinned but said nothing.

Orrie also grinned. "You're not getting paid anything. You're doing it pro bono."

Jack shrugged. "Judge Mack doesn't have any money. As a circuit judge, he didn't get paid much more than a cowhand. But it's for a good cause. The Judge and Miss Angie are good people."

"All right, counsellor, you make a persuasive case. I'm on board. Now, go home and get some sleep. We have a trial to win."

THE SECOND CHANCE WAS once again set up for court. However, this time instead of tables to be used for the Town Council, a chair was behind the bar and the bar would serve as the judge's bench.

Tables were set up for an audience, and standing room was provided at the back. Hunter served coffee and Aunt Ginny brought in breakfast food from the restaurant side. Business on court day was usually hopping.

Tom and Danny escorted Judge Mack in from the jail. Mack's wrists were cuffed in front of him, and he walked with Tom on one side and Danny on the other.

Angie was with them. Tom allowed it but, once they stepped into the Second Chance, he said to her, "You'll need to go sit at a table, Miss Angie. Miss Alisha and Miss Maybelle have saved a chair for you."

"I'll be right here, Judge, right behind you."

"I know you will, Sweetie."

And Angie headed over to Alisha and Maybelle.

The Judge looked at Tom with a grin. "She loves me."

Tom returned the grin. "Can't figure why."

"Me neither."

Orrie stepped in behind them and said, "We might as well sit down."

A table was set up for the legal team representing the defendant, and another for the prosecution. Tom removed the cuffs from the Judge's wrists, and the Judge took one chair.

Orrie pulled out a pocket watch from a vest pocket. "It's almost nine. We'll be starting shortly."

The Judge said, "I hope Jack gets here soon."

Orrie nodded. "He'll be along."

Springer stepped into the room, and Hiram and Quint were with him.

Quint said, "I don't see why we need to be here, if this is gonna be just about picking the jury."

Springer sat down at the table designated for the prosecution and opened an attaché. "In case the judge wants to speak with you or swear you in. The first day of a trial is when any motion for charges to be dismissed might be made. I don't know what tricks McCabe might have in mind."

Judge Mack said to Orrie, "How many people do you think are back there?"

Orrie glanced back. "I think we might have fifty in here."

Mack shook his head. "We never had this many in any case I presided over."

Orrie shrugged his shoulders. "You're a minor celebrity around here, Judge. And it's an unusual case. A judge doesn't usually stand trial himself."

Orrie glanced over his shoulder again. "I think that's Jacob Carlisle, from the Montana Weekly Herald."

Judge Mack shook his head and sat back in his chair. "I just want this fiasco to be over."

Jack came in, wearing a three-piece suit that was charcoal gray with thin, white pinstripes. However, he didn't wear a bowler like many men did when in a suit and tie. He wore a wide-brimmed range hat and on his feet were riding boots.

Springer rose to his feet as Jack passed him. "McCabe, again I must state the obvious, that it is a conflict of interest for you to be representing Judge Mack. It could be easily interpreted as an attempt on your part to gain favor that might benefit you in future cases."

Mack said, "Calm down, Counsellor. I have no intention of serving as judge after this."

"Thank God for small favors."

"I've had enough of you, too, and men like you. Believe me. I've had enough of courtroom theatrics."

Quint looked at Hiram. "Theater what? There ain't no show goin' on in this town."

Hiram said, "Believe me, we *are* the show."

Jack took a chair beside Orrie and opened his brief case. "Thanks again, Orrie."

"Maybe working with you will help me learn something. Gain some of the experience I need."

Judge Mack nodded his head. "Been to law school and served as a circuit judge here in Montana for a number of years. My father was a lawyer back east and a number of his friends were lawyers. Believe me when I say I ain't never seen one better'n Jack."

Jack shook his head. "Judge, you're gonna make me blush."

He pulled out his pocket watch and found it was three past nine. He was about to say the new judge was late when Judge Mather walked in. A bowler covered his white hair, and he stepped behind the bar and set the hat down on it.

Hunter called out, "All rise! The Honorable Judge Barnabas Mather."

Everyone rose. Mather took his seat and everyone sat back down.

Mather looked at Hunter, and Hunter held up a sheet of paper. "Court is now in session. First case on the docket: The People versus Hannibal McIntyre."

One man called out, "It's the only case, Hunter."

And everyone laughed.

Mather banged his gavel on the table. "Order in the court. I will have order or I will clear the courtroom. Does everyone understand?"

Mack said, "If he can get order out of this bunch of yay-hoos, he's a better man than I am."

He said it loud enough to be heard, and there was another round of laughter while Mather banged his gavel again.

Once the laughter died down, Mather looked from Jack to Springer. "Are there any statements either of you would wish to make before we begin jury selection?"

Springer shook his head but Jack rose to his feet. "There is, your Honor."

"Please proceed."

"I move for this case to be dismissed."

"On what ground?"

"On the grounds that the only two witnesses the prosecution has found presented widely different statements."

Springer rose to his feet. "I object, your Honor. My witnesses haven't even been called to the stand yet."

Jack reached into his brief case. "Both witnesses made statements under oath in the Town Council meeting where we voted to file murder charges."

"That was hardly court, your Honor. That was a Town Council meeting. Nothing said there can be admissible in a court of law."

Jack held up some sheets of paper. "Those men were under oath, your Honor. I would like to submit into evidence this transcript of those proceedings, as taken by my assistant, Miss Myrna Warren."

Mather held out his hand. "Bring the evidence forward."

Jack did.

"Is Miss Warren present?

She was at a table behind the defense table. She rose to her feet. "Right here, your Honor."

"Come forward please."

She did.

Judge Mather handed the papers to her. "Do these papers constitute the transcript you took from the Town Council meeting?"

"They sure do, Judge." She handed them back to him.

"All right. I will need some time to review the evidence. Court will adjourn and reconvene tomorrow morning at nine o'clock sharp." He tapped down his gavel.

"What?" one man called out. "We just got ourselves sat down."

Mather drove his gavel onto the top of the bar and nearly shouted. "I will have order in this court!"

Everyone was silent. He then rose to his feet and Hunter called out, "Everyone rise."

They did, to a shuffle of shoe and boot soles and the sliding of wooden chair legs.

Hunter called out, "Court is adjourned. Bar's open, boys."

That got some shouts of approval and the crowd swarmed the bar.

Quint leaned over to Hiram. "What's all that mean?"

"It means the Judge is going to review our statements from the Town Council meeting. If he agrees with Jack that our statements don't match, which they don't, then he might approve Jack's motion to dismiss the case."

"I've gotta do something about that cousin of yours."

"What? What do you mean?"

"You leave it to me."

Hiram decided to take his chances one more time with a dinner at the Cattleman's. He took a table and the woman he was coming to know as Miss Maybelle came over.

She said, "Isn't there someplace else in town where you can eat?"

He looked at her. "Your customer service is exquisite."

The room was about half full and some of the patrons looked over at him uncomfortably, as though they smelled something bad.

"Look," he said to her. "I'm a paying customer, no different than anyone else."

"There is one difference. No one else in the room is trying to get Judge Mack hanged for murder."

He sat back in his chair with resignation. "Neither am I. I'm just testifying as to what I saw."

"Are you really? And just what did you see? Angie Thacker is like family around here. Judge Mack saved her life, and your testimony might send him to the gallows. Do you call that justice?"

"I don't know what I call it." His head was spinning a little with everything that was going on. Dealing with Quint and his threats was tiring. "May I please see a menu?"

"I don't think so."

Miss Alisha came over. "Maybelle, this man harassing you again?"

Maybelle nodded her head. "Mm-hmm."

Hiram shook his head wearily. "I'm not harassing anyone. I just want to eat dinner."

"And get a good friend of ours hanged."

Hiram hung his head. He wanted to bang his head against the table. "Could I please see a menu?"

Alisha shook her head. "No."

"Then I'll take the same thing I had before. Steak and baked potatoes."

"How much money do you have?"

"So it's going to be like that."

"You can always go elsewhere. They serve dinner at the Second Chance and Johansen's."

He shook his head. "I think I'm even more reviled at the Second Chance than I am here, and Johansen's is across town."

"The Randall House serves dinner."

"That's where I'm staying. Have you ever eaten there? I'd be better off buying a can of beans at the general store and eating them cold."

Maybelle looked at Alisha. "He has a point."

Alisha said, "The Golden Nugget serves steak."

Hiram shook his head. "Would you actually eat there? I don't like even stepping in there. I'm afraid a louse or a flea might jump on me."

Alisha said, "How much money do you have?"

He reached into his jacket for his wallet and produced two more twenties. "Will this do?"

Alisha snagged the twenties. "It's a start."

"Could you include a glass of merlot?"

"Maybe."

"And could you ask the chef not to spit on the steak?"

Alisha held out her hand. Hiram gave a huffing sigh, shook his head and handed her a ten dollar bill. "This is all I have. I'll have to go to the bank tomorrow."

Alisha took the bill. "All right. No spitting."

Hiram ate his meal in silence, and it was dark by the time he reached the hotel. As he approached the door to his room, he saw two men coming out of Quint's doorway. They were in miner's clothes and stood taller than he. One was muscled like a man who did hard work for a living and the other had a fat face and a round stomach.

They walked past Hiram and one shouldered him off to the side as he passed.

Quint followed them out but only as far as Hiram's door.

Hiram said, "Who are those two?"

"Men I just hired."

"To do what?"

"A job. None of your concern. Let's go downstairs and order us a bottle of whiskey."

"I have no money left, until I go to the bank tomorrow. Those fifty dollar meals at the Cattleman's are draining my funds."

"The barkeep will give us credit. I'm sure you're good for it."

Jack pulled up a stool outside Judge Mack's cell.

Mack said, "Shouldn't you be home?"

Jack nodded. "Just had dinner, but I wanted to check on you."

Angie sat in a chair next to the cell door. "What do you think'll happen tomorrow?"

"I don't like to make predictions. Wouldn't want to jinx the case. But I think I made a good case today for a dismissal."

The Judge nodded his head. "I think you would have persuaded me."

Angie looked worried. "But what if the judge don't dismiss the case? What then?"

"Then we proceed with the trial. We select a jury, which might take a week. And then I tear apart both witnesses on the stand."

Mack nodded. "I've seen you do it, and I've never seen two witnesses who had more holes in their stories."

Angie didn't seem convinced. "But what if you can't? What if that Springer feller objects, or whatever they do?"

Jack shook his head. "You, Miss Angie, are a pessimist."

"I am not." She looked at the Judge. "What does that mean?"

He grinned. "It means you see the worst or fear the worst in every situation."

"Oh." She looked at Jack. "Maybe I am."

Jack left the jail and headed back toward home. It was dark and even though some of the cities back east were using street lights, and Jack had read in the paper that even San Francisco and Los Angeles had them, he figured it would be a long time before a small remote town the size of Jubilee got them. Even still, the moon cast enough light that he could see up and down the street.

It was a Thursday night and things were slow in this town at this time of the week. The boardwalks were empty and so was the street. The only sign of life he could see was a couple of horses outside the Second Chance.

He walked along. While he was not wearing a gun on his hip, a shoulder holster was in place. Normally he wouldn't expect trouble on a sleepy Thursday evening in Jubilee, but after what had almost happened to Em, and Dusty being shot, he thought it was wise to have a gun on him.

Even still, he wasn't paying attention as he should have been. His mind was on the court trial, and what to do if Judge Mather refused to dismiss the case. He crossed the street and walked past the building that had in the early days of this town been Miss Alisha's establishment. Back before she gave up her previous business and became a restauranteur.

As he walked past the alley between the old building and a jewelry store next to it, a man stepped out from the alley and into the moonlight, a pistol in his hand.

"Hold it right there, McCabe. Hands where I can see 'em."

Dang, Jack thought. *Let him get the jump on me.*

Jack lifted his hands into the air. "I have twelve dollars in my wallet. That's all."

"We don't want your money, McCabe. Into the alleyway. Get moving."

Jack shook his head. "No."

The man took a step closer and raised his gun to the level of Jack's face. "I ain't playin' games. Get into the alley."

"Nope. Can't do it."

"Why not?"

"I'm afraid of the dark."

Apparently the man didn't find Jack amusing. "You get into that alley or I'll put a bullet into you."

"Do you have a horse ready?"

The man dropped his brows into a frown. "Huh?"

"A gunshot is going to bring people running. The marshal's office is only a short walk from here, and my father and Uncle Matt are working for him. One of them is almost always out walking their rounds. Believe me, you put a bullet in me, you don't want to be caught by my father or Uncle Matt. So you'd be wise to have a horse waiting for you out behind the alley. Beyond these buildings is open range, and if you try to escape on foot out there, you're not going to make it. So to shoot me down with no horse waiting for you is stupid."

A man spoke from the alley. "Will you tell him to shut up and get in here?"

The first man looked back over his shoulder. "He might have a point. We ain't got no horses."

Taking his eyes off of Jack was a mistake, which the man found out as Jack launched at him. With one hand he grabbed the man's gunhand by the wrist, and with the other he drove his fingers straight toward the man's eyes. A trick Bree had shown him that she had learned from Mister Chen.

His fingers missed the man's eyes and hit the bridge of his nose and the edge of an eye socket, but it caused the man to close his eyes and turn his head, which was actually the desired reaction.

Jack gripped the man's wrist now with both hands and brought the wrist down over one knee, like he was breaking a stick. The gun came loose from the man's grasp.

Jack then planted his feet and drove two hard punches into the man's stomach. Jack had done some boxing in college and still worked out once a week at the ranch, driving his fists into a burlap sack filled with sand and hay and suspended from a barn rafter by a rope. It paid off as both punches hit like sledge hammers, and the man doubled up and fell backward.

The second man emerged from the alley, a knife in one hand, and he drove it toward Jack's midsection. Jack stepped back and away, but not fast enough and the blade cut into his ribs.

He thought about grabbing the gun in his shoulder holster, but he didn't have enough time. The man looked like he had fought with a knife before and knew what he was doing. His feet were placed far enough apart for balance but not too far, and he began slashing and lunging at Jack.

Jack's hat was still in place, so he pulled it off and threw it at the man. The attacker swatted the hat away, but it gave Jack the time he needed to pull his .38.

The man raised his knife to throw it at Jack, but Jack was cocking the revolver as he drew it and placed a bullet directly between the man's eyes.

The first man was on his feet and grabbed his gun from where it had fallen in the dirt. Jack fired from the hip, placing a bullet in the man's chest. The man staggered back two steps but kept his balance, and he raised his gun for a shot.

Jack fired again, this time into the man's forehead. The attacker's head snapped back and his knees were suddenly made of rubber, and he went down.

Jack heard footsteps—someone was running toward him from behind. He turned, bringing his gun up for another shot, but he saw it was Uncle Matt, scattergun in hand.

"Jack? That you?"

Jack nodded. "These two jumped me from the alley."

The second attacker still held a gun in his grip, so Matt pulled the gun free and then placed two fingers onto his neck to check for a pulse. "He's dead."

"So's the other one." Jack pulled a handkerchief from one jacket pocket and pressed it against the slice along his ribs.

"Hey, you're bleeding."

Jack nodded. "The one with the knife got me. Not bad, I don't think."

"Looks like you're bleeding a lot. Come on, let's get to Doc Martin's office. It'll take too long for Haley to get here."

25

THE NEXT MORNING, Jack shouldered into a white shirt. A white bandage that was unintentionally matching was wrapped about his ribs.

Nina stood in the doorway to their bedroom. "How does it feel?"

"It didn't hurt much last night, but now it kind of stings."

It wasn't unusual to hear a horse go by the house, or a horse and wagon. But Jack thought he heard a horse and wagon directly beneath their bedroom window, and a man saying, "Whoa."

"Sounds like someone's outside."

Nina went to the window. "Oh. It's Haley. Looks like Charles is with her. You keep getting dressed. I'll go let them in."

Jack came downstairs, putting the finishing touches on his tie, and he found Haley waiting for him.

"I want to have a look at that knife wound."

He shook his head. "It'll be all right. I have to be at the Second Chance in half an hour for court."

"Did Doc Martin apply honey to the wound?"

He shook his head. "But he did a good job cleaning it out and applying sutures."

"Come into the kitchen. I want a look at it."

Nina said to Haley, "He said it was stinging this morning."

Haley nodded her head. "An early sign of infection. Jack, come with us to the kitchen."

Nina looked at him. "You have Orrie Scott assisting you. I'm sure he can handle things until you get there."

Charles said, "I'll head over to the marshal's office and tell them you might be a little late."

Judge Mather strode into the Second Chance and Hunter bellowed out, "Court is now in session. The

Honorable Judge Mather presiding."

Mather placed his bowler on the bar and sat.

And Jack came in through the batwing doors. Nina was with him, along with Haley and Charles.

Mather looked at him through spectacles perched on his nose. "Nice of you to join us, Counsellor. I hope it wasn't too much of a bother to be here, *almost* on time."

"I'm sorry, Your Honor. Won't happen again."

Tom McCabe and his father had brought the prisoner to court this morning. Danny and Johnny were patrolling.

Tom stepped forward. "Your Honor, may I address the court?"

Mather scowled at him. "This is highly irregular."

"Yes, sir, it certainly is. But last night, Counsel for the defense, Jackson McCabe, was attacked on the streets of our town and sustained a knife wound."

Mather looked at Jack. "Is this so?"

Jack nodded. "Yes, Your Honor, but I'll be all right. My doctor insisted on follow-up treatment before I got here. That's why I'm late."

"In light of the incident against..." he lifted a sheet of paper and glanced at his notes, "...one Emma McCabe, could this be in any way connected?"

"Unknown at this time, Your Honor." Jack placed his briefcase on the table used for the Defense.

Hiram and Quint sat immediately behind the prosecutor's table. Hiram's gaze was toward the floor, and he shook his head and muttered, "This can't go on. It has to stop."

Quint said to him, "Shut up."

Mather said to Jack, "Could this be in any way connected to this trial?"

"Also unknown."

Judge Mack chuckled. "You know it is."

Mather looked at his notes again. "Could you be related to the Miss McCabe in question?"

Jack nodded his head. "I could be very well, and indeed am. She's my sister."

"I see."

Hiram jumped to his feet. "No. this cannot go any further."

Quint looked up at him. "Sit down."

"Your Honor, if I may approach the bench, I need to inform you and the Marshal of what has been going on."

Quint gritted his teeth. "Sit...down!"

Judge Mather looked at Hiram. "This is also highly irregular."

"That's how my life has been lately." Hiram approached the bench. "Your Honor, the attack on Jack McCabe and on his sister Emma, and the shooting of Dusty McCabe out at the ranch a few days ago, was all caused by that man."

He turned and pointed a finger at Quint.

Quint rose to his feet. "You're a dead man."

Hiram went on. "He hired those men to attack the McCabe girl, and he hired additional men to attack the defense counsel last night. He laid in wait and shot Dusty McCabe out at the ranch. And he told me to say nothing of any of this on the threat of death. He instructed me to lie on the witness stand during the Town Council meeting, also on the threat of death."

"Is that so?"

Quint pulled his gun and aimed it toward Tom. "Keep your hands where they are, lawman."

And Quint ran for the door.

"Stop him!" the judge called out.

And Quint ran directly into the fist of Johnny McCabe.

Johnny had stopped in the doorway of the Second Chance, taking a break from walking his rounds. His knuckles caught Quint squarely in the right brow, and Quint was stopped as though he had run into a wall. Quint's feet went out from under him and he landed on his back.

Johnny yanked the gun from his grip and then aimed the scattergun at his face. "Do I have to tell you that you're under arrest?"

"Nope. Figured that out on my own."

Johnny pulled Quint to his feet. Tom put cuffs on Quint, and Johnny said to the marshal, "I'll take him to the jail. You should be here with your father and Hiram."

Since they were already in court, Mather requested that Hiram take the witness stand. Hunter swore him in, and then Jack began asking questions. "Why were you sent here to Jubilee?"

"My employer, Aloysius Randall, wants to obtain some commercial properties in the area, including the McCabe Ranch. I was here to scout out the various properties and make the owners cash offers. Including an offer on the ranch."

He went on to describe Quint's function in all of it. He talked and held nothing back.

Mather looked at Jack. "I'm going to have to wire the Attorney General of California. He might want to ask this Aloysius Randall a few questions."

Hiram continued talking. He told of how he had received an offer three years earlier from Aloysius Randall to merge both of their businesses together.

"He took all of Virginia Middleton's assets. Those assets were quite formidable, and he was able to take them all. And I did nothing to stop it. I'm so sorry."

Jack thought it sounded more like Hiram was confessing to a priest than giving testimony. And maybe confessing was indeed what he was doing. Confessing before God Almighty and everyone in the room.

Matt stepped in and went over to stand beside Jack. Courtroom protocol was pretty much dismissed at this point.

Hiram looked at Matt. "I'm so sorry, Father. All I wanted at first was to make you and Mother proud. And then when it became clear you weren't with Mother on her business decisions and her way of doing things, she told me you were weak and I was not to be like you. I tried so hard to be strong, Father." He shook his head and tears ran down his face. "I tried so hard. But I didn't know what *strong* was. It turns out you were the strong one all along."

Matt walked over and placed a hand on Hiram's shoulder, and Hiram sat on the witness chair with his head bowed and wept silently.

Mather looked at Springer. "I think it's safe to say there will be no charges of perjury filed against him."

Springer stood and shook his head. "No, Your Honor."

Judge Mather tapped his gavel on the bar. "Case dismissed."

26

JOHNNY FOUND Matt and Tom with Hiram, at the Second Chance. The crowd had dispersed and the three had taken a table.

Tom looked at Johnny. "Is the prisoner secured?"

Johnny nodded his head. "Secured, and with a black eye. He's in Judge Mack's former cell, and Danny's in the office."

Hiram looked exhausted. His face had no color and dark circles had formed under his eyes. He looked like he hadn't slept in weeks. Maybe he hadn't, Johnny thought.

Johnny now saw that Hiram had been carrying a lot of conflicting emotion, probably for most of his life.

Hiram said, "Quint's where he should be. Where he can't hurt anyone anymore."

Matt looked at Hiram. "Son, I'd like to buy you something to eat, at the restaurant side of this place."

Hiram shook his head. "Thanks, Father, but I think I'd like to just go back to my hotel room and be alone for a while."

Matt nodded, and he watched as Hiram got to his feet and walked across the room toward the door, his head lowered.

Quint stretched out on the cot in his cell. Nathan Springer stood outside the barred door.

"Mister Quint, I still have to research the situation and decide on what charges will be filed. But, believe me, there will be charges."

Quint flipped a hand in the air, as if to say, *Yeah? So?*

Springer said, "You might want to take this matter seriously. Do you deny hiring men to launch a violent attack on Emma McCabe? Do you deny hiring men in an attempt to have Jack McCabe murdered?"

"I ain't denyin' nothin'."

"So, you're confessing?"

"Ain't confessing to nothing neither."

Springer let out a sigh of frustration. "Mister Quint, you might seriously consider getting yourself an attorney."

"Who?" He grinned. "Jack McCabe?"

"He's not the only attorney in town. There is also Origen Scott."

"That idjit? Judge Mack would have been sent to the gallows if he had kept him on as his lawyer, and Mack didn't even do anything wrong."

Tom McCabe stood in the cell block doorway. "Doesn't look like you're getting anywhere with him."

Springer looked at Quint. "Maybe you'll take things more seriously when charges are filed."

Quint flipped a hand in the air again.

Tom said to Springer, "You've done all you can."

Quint sat up on the cot and swung his legs over the side. "You know what your problem is, Counsellor? Jealousy. You're jealous of them McCabes, just like one schoolboy on the playground being jealous of another. This case of yours against Judge Mack was proof of it. You almost made my job a lot easier, because I was hired to kill Judge Mack, among other things. If you got him hanged, you'd be doing my job for me. But what it comes down to is you're jealous of them McCabes. Pure and simple."

Springer glared at him. He wanted to respond with something clever. Something biting. But he couldn't find the words.

He turned on his heel and strode out of the cell block.

Quint laughed long and hard.

Hiram sat at a table at the Cattleman's, with a plate of food in front of him. He thought he might try a ham this time, and he had a glass of white wine. The bottle stood on the table in front of him.

Jack and Matt stepped in, and they walked over

to the table.

"Hiram," Matt said. "You did the right thing today."

Hiram looked at him. "I was sitting in my room, staring at the walls, and I decided maybe I didn't want to be alone after all. But I came here because I didn't really feel like talking to anyone."

Matt said, "I understand."

"You didn't think I had it in me, did you? To do the right thing."

Matt said nothing.

"Well, I'll soon be out of your hair. I'm heading back to California. A train leaves for San Francisco tomorrow, and I plan to be on it. I plan to have a talk with Aloysius Randall. It's time our business partnership was dissolved."

"Be careful," Jack said. "He's a snake."

"So I'm becoming aware."

Hiram lifted his glass of wine for a sip. "People are no longer treating me like I'm the living incarnation of evil. Miss Alisha charged me only a normal price for this meal, and now you're all speaking to me. Maybe I'm not the monster you all thought I was."

Jack nodded. "Maybe you're right."

He looked at Matt. "I'll leave you two to talk. I'm going to see if Judge Mack is here."

Jack headed to the staircase, and Matt said to Hiram, "Mind if I sit?"

Hiram motioned a hand toward a chair and Matt slid it out and dropped into it.

"Hiram, I know you don't want to talk, so I'll do the talking. I owe you an apology."

"No you don't. I've never been a very good man. Not really."

"What I'm sorry for is not being more available to you when you were growing up. It's hard to explain what happened. I'm not sure I understand it myself."

Hiram said nothing. He took a bite of ham.

Matt shrugged his shoulders. "Your mother was

evil. No question about that."

Hiram was about to object. But then he thought better of it. After all, he felt he knew Mother better than anyone. "I think she meant well. In her own warped way."

Hiram raised a hand for a waitress. A young woman he had not seen before. "Could we have another glass?"

She brought over a second goblet and Hiram filled it with wine and slid it over to his father.

"So tell me, Father. What reason did you possibly have for marrying her?"

"I was young. Foolish. Thought I was in love." Matt shrugged his shoulders. "Maybe I was. In love with the girl I thought she was. In love with an illusion only I could see."

He took a sip of wine. "When you were born, she was almost strangely possessive of you. She insisted you be raised in a certain way, and she wanted to oversee it."

He sat back in his chair, and his gaze grew distant. "I allowed it, because she seemed so sophisticated and learned in the finer walks of life. As the years went by, I began to see her more for who she was, but I suppose I wanted to hang onto the illusion. She spent little time with Tom or Danny, and I taught them what I knew. How to survive in the wilderness, and how to judge livestock, how to brand a calf, how to break a horse. I was quite good at riding a bucking bronc in my youth."

Hiram blinked with surprise. "I never knew that."

Matt nodded. "When Johnny and our brother Joe and I first rode onto the ranch that would later become your mother's and mine, it was run by your grandfather."

Hiram nodded. "Frank McCarty. He died before I was old enough to remember."

"I rode in with my two brothers and we got hired as cowhands. It wasn't long before your Uncle Johnny was the ramrod. Or cow boss. That's what we called it in those days. He has a natural leadership quality that people gravitate toward.

"Then I got the notion into my head that I wanted to specialize in breaking wild horses. That was in the old days, before Johnny spent time with the Shoshone and learned their way of breaking a horse. At the time, I wanted to impress your mother and I thought the only way I could do it was by doing a foolhardy stunt like staying in the saddle of a wild, bucking horse."

Hiram grinned. "Were you any good?"

Matt nodded. "Strangely, yes. I became one of the top bronc busters on the ranch."

"I never knew that. Did you ever get injured?"

Matt nodded again. "Oh, yeah. More than once. I cracked some ribs a couple of times. Got a shoulder separated once. My left knee still hurts when it's going to rain and both knees snap and crackle if I kneel down."

"My father, the bronc buster."

Matt grinned. "I got into the foolish game simply to impress your mother, but after a time, I came to take pride in it. I could remain in the saddle longer than anyone else on the ranch. We would have competitions with other ranches. Rodeos, we sometimes called them. I won the bronc busting contests more than once."

Hiram was intrigued. "How is it Mother never told me anything about this?"

Matt shrugged. "For reasons I can't even begin to guess, she wanted you for herself. She might have decided not to tell you about me because she didn't want you learning from me, like Tom and Danny did. I don't think she wanted you in the saddle, riding night herd and such."

"Tell me. What was it like to be on the back of one of those wild, bucking horses?"

Matt smiled with wonder. "It feels like the most dangerous thing on Earth. Like you're flirting with death and your life is hanging by a thread. And yet, somehow,

I never felt more alive..."

Jack knocked on a door upstairs, and Judge Mack opened it. "Jack. Come on in."

Jack found Angie packing a trunk.

She looked at him with a beaming smile. "The Judge has asked me to marry him."

Jack smiled. "I assume this is a good thing?"

"Oh, yes. And I said yes. I've dreamed of this moment."

"So..." Jack looked at the trunk. "You're leaving?"

The Judge nodded his head. "We're gonna get a fresh start, somewheres else."

"Do you have any idea where?"

He shrugged his shoulders. "Idaho's nice. And I hear people are looking at Alaska. Might be open to settlement soon."

"Alaska? What's up there?"

"Nothing. No people. And that's why we like the idea of it."

Angie looked at Jack. "No one to judge you, thinking you're not good enough because you ain't never been to school. Or not pretty enough, or not good enough."

The Judge said, "Angie, sweetie, you're the prettiest gal I ever did meet. You don't let no one ever tell you that you ain't pretty. Or good enough."

"Miss Angie," Jack said, "I think you are one of the most impressive people I have ever met."

She gave him a smile. "Jack, you'll never know how much that means to me."

The Judge put an arm around her shoulders. "This here is the gal I want to spend the rest of my life with."

She said, "I don't know how to ride a horse, but the Judge said we can buy a wagon."

"I got me some money saved up."

Jack couldn't help but smile. And yet, he had to admit he would miss these two. "So, you've resigned your judgeship?"

Mack shook his head. "The governor'll figure it out, sooner or later."

Jack grinned.

There was another knock at the door. The door was still open, and Tom McCabe was in the doorway, actually knocking on the door jamb. "I hate to interrupt, but I just wanted to check in on you two."

The Judge smiled. "Marshal, you showed up at just the right time. We were hoping you would do us a favor, not in your position as marshal but in your former position as preacher. From what the new preacher in town has told us, you're still officially ordained."

Tom nodded. "So it would seem."

Angie said, "We would be honored if you would marry us, Marshal."

"I would be honored to. Do you have a date in mind?"

Judge Mack nodded. "Yep. First of tomorrow."

"Tomorrow?"

"Yessir. We want to be married as soon as possible."

Angie chimed in. "We don't want to wait another minute. What almost happened to the Judge, being found guilty of a murder he didn't really do and maybe being hanged for it, well it makes us realize the time we have together is precious."

The Judge nodded. "We want to get married and start our new lives together, as soon as possible."

Tom nodded his head and couldn't help but smile. "I would be honored to officiate at your wedding."

Angie looked at the Judge. "I just love it when he and Jack use words like that."

It was growing dark when Matt swung into the saddle. He looked down at Tom, who was standing on the boardwalk. "Well, Marshal, it's been quite a day."

"That it has, Father. I don't think I'll be needing

you or Uncle Johnny anymore as deputies, but I wanted to thank you for helping out."

"Anytime. Just let me know."

"I will. And say hello to Peddie for me."

"I'll do that." Matt turned his horse and rode down the street at a slow walk.

Tom began the walk from the livery stable to his office, the heels of his boots thunking along the boardwalk. He thought he might order dinner from the Second Chance and then afterward stop by the house and have a few moments with Mercy and Hilly. And then he would go back to the office and spell Danny. His brother had been working long hours during the trial of Judge Mack, and Tom thought he might give him the night off.

Tom stepped into the office. Danny wasn't at his desk, and the door to the cell block was open.

"Danny?"

No answer. Tom crossed the room to the cell block and found Danny face down on the floor. The cell door was open and Quint was gone.

Tom knelt by Danny's side and rolled him over, and found he was still breathing.

"Danny, can you hear me?"

Danny's eyes fluttered and he coughed. He brought one hand to his forehead and Tom saw a bruise was forming.

"Danny, what happened?"

Danny shook his head. "Let him get the jump on me. He called for me, so I came in and found the cell door open. He hit me hard with a coffee cup. Never seen a coffee cup used as a weapon before."

Tom saw a blue speckled coffee cup on the floor. It was dented, from where it had apparently made contact with Danny's head.

Danny said, "I'm so sorry, Tom. I let him get away."

27

HIRAM PUSHED a key into the lock of his hotel room
door, turned the keys so the tumblers clicked, and he
pushed the door open.

The room was dark because Hiram was not one to
leave a kerosene lamp burning low while he was gone.
He knew many who did that, so if they returned after
dark there would be a low level of light in the room. But
he hated the smell of kerosene smoke and sure didn't
want to come into a room that was filled with it, so he
used a lamp only when he needed to.

The lamp was on the chest of drawers against one
wall. The chest where he had often stood a bottle of
whiskey he was working on.

He walked over, lifted the glass chimney, and
struck a match to bring the lamp to life. Then he set the
chimney back in place, and he pulled the short-barreled
revolver he carried from an inside jacket pocket and set
it on the chest.

The gun was a Smith and Wesson Model One,
which came in a .22 caliber. Not a very large bullet, but
he found it was fine for close-range shooting. And it
didn't matter the size of the bullet, he remembered
hearing Father say to Tom years ago, if you place the
bullet in the right spot. He set the gun on the chest by
the lamp.

He always carried a gun. After all, he was a
McCabe. Not really, he supposed, and he had received
little of Father's teachings when he was growing up. But
he had received enough to know you were always
prepared. You carried matches with you, and a good
sharp knife, and you had a gun.

He began to turn away from the chest when he
heard the voice. A voice he had hoped never to hear
again. "Howdy, city boy."

Quint was sitting on the bed. In his hand was a
.45 and it was aimed at Hiram.

"I thought you were in jail."

Quint nodded. "Was. But there ain't a jail in these little cow towns that can hold me. I learned long ago to carry something like this with me."

In his left hand was a thin strip of metal. "Works like a skeleton key. All you have to do is push it into the lock and turn them little tumbler things. It's how I got out of the cell and how I got into this here room."

He chuckled. "That deputy learned a hard lesson tonight. If he lives. I hit him durn hard."

"That deputy is my brother."

Quint shrugged his shoulders. "Don't matter none. One less McCabe in the world."

"And so you sat in the dark and waited for me."

"Knew you'd come back sooner or later. Couldn't have the lamp on. Didn't want no one outside and down below to see a lighted window up here."

He got up from the bed and walked over toward the door. Hiram hoped it would mean Quint was leaving, but then he realized all Quint was doing was positioning himself between the door and Hiram.

Hiram realized he wasn't frightened. If anything, he was weary. Weary of it all. "What do you want?"

Quint pushed the gun into the front of his pants. He was wearing no gunbelt. Hiram figured Quint must have taken the gun from Danny and didn't have time to reclaim his own rig before escaping from the marshal's office.

Quint said, "Remember what I told you I would do if you didn't do like you was supposed to?"

Hiram said nothing.

Quint reached down to one boot and pulled a long knife.

Hiram's eyes were on the blade. "Where'd you get that?"

"From a plate on the deputy's desk. Food he got delivered from the Second Chance. This here is a steak knife."

"That's bigger than any steak knife I've ever seen."

"A little bigger, maybe. But it only looks real big because you know I'm gonna kill you with it."

Quint began walking toward him. "I told you I was gonna stick you like a pig and watch you bleed out on the floor. Now you get to see what that feels like. You'll die slow and painful. I plan to be long gone before they find your body."

Hiram thought his one chance to survive was his revolver. He lunged for it, but Quint was faster than Hiram thought he would be. Hiram got his hand on the gun but Quint grabbed him by the wrist.

They struggled for a moment, Hiram trying to bring the gun down toward the level of Quint's face. But the gun wasn't cocked, and it couldn't be fired otherwise because it was a single-action. Hiram found he couldn't manage to cock it while trying to out-muscle Quint.

As they were struggling, Quint drove the knife into Hiram's midsection. It went deep.

Hiram stopped, his eyes wide and his mouth hanging open.

Quint grinned, and he pulled the knife free. "Pulling the knife out will make you bleed faster."

Hiram staggered a step backward, the gun in his hand now forgotten.

Quint grabbed the gun with his free hand pulled it from Hiram's grip. Hiram looked down at his white shirt to see a patch of blood red growing.

"You'll die," Quint said. "And now you know what it feels like to be stuck like a pig. Figure you'll last a half hour or so, on the floor in this room, dying in misery. That's what you get for trying to stand against Mister Randall. When you stand against him, you lose. Thought you'd have figured that out by now."

Hiram looked at him, more with surprise than anything else. Then he fell to his knees.

Quint was still grinning. "Only thing I feel bad about is I can't wait around and watch you die. I've still got work to do for Mister Randall. I've gotta get out of Montana, but when I ride away, the McCabe ranch house will be going up in flames."

He went to the door and pulled it open. "So long, city boy."

Quint headed toward the back stairs that would come out in the kitchen. He had to have a plan, and one quickly formed in his mind. He would wait out the night in the woods outside of town. Then, in the morning, he would make his way to the McCabe ranch. But to do all of that, he would need food and a horse.

He could smell something good coming from the kitchen as he descended the stairs, and he figured it would take care of his concern for food.

He stepped down and into the kitchen, and found a cook at work in front of the stove. The cook was in a white shirt and apron, and he was frying up a steak in a skillet.

The man looked at him, a man stepping out of the stairwell with a gun in one hand a knife in the other.

"Wait," the man said. "Who are you? What do you want?"

Quint didn't hesitate. He strode across the kitchen and shoved the knife deep into the man, just under his rib cage.

He had stabbed Hiram in a way that would let him die slowly, but he had to silence this man immediately. Quint knew a knife blade just under the ribs and driven up a little would make it so you couldn't breathe, so that was what he aimed for. He drove the knife in and upward, deep and hard, and the cook went up on his toes trying to back away from Quint.

Quint followed him along, keeping the knife in place. The man's mouth opened but no words came. Quint then pulled the knife free and the man fell to the floor.

The man was trying to breathe but his lungs wouldn't work. Good enough for Quint. He tucked Hiram's revolver into his belt beside the one he had taken from the deputy. And he wiped the knife on the cook's shirt, wiping away the blood from both stabbings.

A burlap sack was draped over a nail in one wall, and Quint grabbed it. He tipped the skillet into the sack. A loaf of bread was in the oven and looked nearly done, so he dumped that into the sack, too.

He glanced down at the cook. The man's hands were pressed over the wound and he was trying to suck in air with lungs that no longer worked. Quint figured the man had only moments of consciousness left.

"Thanks for the vittles," Quint said. "Now I gotta go find me a horse."

And then he pulled open the door and ran out into the dark alley.

Hiram decided he was too stubborn to die on his hotel floor. Mother had raised him not to be a victim, and he had heard Father give the same lessons to Tom and Danny.

He crawled across the floor, the front of his shirt now soaking with blood.

He reached up and grasped the door handle and pulled the door open. The hardest thing he had ever done in his life. Then he crawled out and into the corridor.

He heard voices downstairs. A man's voice at the front desk. And a woman's. Hiram tried to call out to them but his voice was nothing more than a croaking whisper, so he crawled.

He crawled to the top of the stairs, and he just let himself fall face forward. It was hard to keep himself from toppling over, so he just let it happen. He went down the stairs, picking up momentum as he went, feeling little as the world spiraled around him. He came to a stop at the bottom of the stairs.

A woman screamed, and that was all he remembered.

Tom and the new minister sat in the marshal's office. They had taken a kettle of coffee over to Second

Chance to be brewed, because the heat of the stove in the small office would have turned the room into a sweatbox. Tom sat at his desk with a tin cup in one hand, and the Reverend Colter was at Danny's desk. He had filled a cup and set it on the desk.

Colter was now in a black clerical shirt and a white collar, and dress pants. And he had shaved.

Tom said, "I'll get a posse together to go after Quint in the morning, but I suspect he's long gone."

He took a sip of coffee. "According to Doc Martin, Danny should be back on his feet in a couple of days. If he's not, I'll call in Haley."

"Just who is this Haley? I've heard the name mentioned."

"Dusty's wife. Dusty is Johnny's son."

Colter nodded. "I've heard the name Dusty McCabe over the years."

"His wife Haley is a folk doctor. What some call a granny woman. The woods are a pharmacy to her. Roots and herbs that cure one thing or another."

"Does that stuff actually work? Sounds like a witch doctor to me."

Tom nodded. "I'll admit, I was a little skeptical at first but, yes, I've seen it work. And Uncle Johnny is convinced and so is my father, and they're both intelligent men."

Colter took a sip of coffee. "Look, if you need any extra help until Danny's back, I can lend a hand."

Tom grinned. "Careful, Pastor. You might find yourself walking the same path I did."

Colter shook his head. "I think I'm walking an opposite path. I began as a soldier and then became something of a gunfighter, but my path led to the ministry."

Tom nodded.

Colter took another sip of coffee. "So, tell me more about Emma McCabe."

Tom's brows rose and he grinned. "Em?"

Colter shrugged. "I have to admit, she has me

intrigued."

Before another word could be said, the door opened and a man charged in. It was Hank Chalmers, the bartender at the hotel lounge. "Marshal. Come quick. It's your brother Hiram. He's been stabbed with a knife, and it looks bad."

Tom and Colter followed Chalmers to the hotel. They found Hiram on the floor at the foot of the stairs. One of the chamber maids was pressing a towel against a wound just beneath Hiram's ribs.

Hiram was conscious, and he looked up at Tom and smiled. "Tom. You're here. Looks like I'm going to meet my end in this dreadful little town."

"What happened?"

"Quint. He was waiting for me in my hotel room. I guess your jail couldn't hold him."

Tom nodded his head. "That's the way of it. He got out and clouted Danny over the head and got away. Danny should be fine but he'll be laid up for a couple of days."

Hiram's voice was weak and his face had lost all color. "Quint ran a knife through me. It was eight inches long and he pushed it in to the hilt. I don't mind dying. I'm sure there are people here who wouldn't mind seeing me gone. Even people in my own family. I just regret that I couldn't do more with my life. Something meaningful."

Tom knelt down by Hiram's side. "Don't talk like that. No one wants to see you gone."

"Really? That's not the way you sounded back in California, when you threatened to kill me."

Tom gave a little sigh. "That was a long time ago."

"I didn't send those men to hurt you or your family. That wasn't my intention."

Doc Martin had been sent for and he came running into the lobby. Tom and the woman got out of the way so he could have a look at the wound.

Colter said, "What do you think, Doc?"

"He's bleeding badly, but I don't think any major

arteries were cut or he'd already be dead."

Hiram nodded wearily. "That was Quint's intention. He wanted me to die slowly and in misery. But you know what? I really don't feel a thing. I feel rather numb all over."

"If we could get in there and tie off the bleeders, he might have a chance."

Tom looked at him. "Can you do it, Doc?"

He shook his head. "Not me. I don't have the knowledge or the experience."

Then he looked up, like a man who had a sudden thought. "Someone run and get Jack McCabe."

Tom and the new preacher waited at the Second Chance. Matt and Peddie stood with them—Tom had thought to send a rider out to his father's cabin. Aunt Ginny and Sam were also there, and Hunter. Aunt Ginny had thought to send a rider out to the ranch, and Johnny had come in.

Harlan Carter stood with them. He had heard the rider going by, on his way to the McCabe Ranch, and when the rider and Johnny were heading back the other way, Harlan flagged them down to ask what the fuss was about.

Hunter opened the bar but all anyone wanted was coffee, so Aunt Ginny got the stove in the restaurant kitchen fired up again and put on a kettle.

Tom had a cup in one hand. "As soon as we know if Hiram is going to make it, we're going to have to form a posse. I figured Quint would be long gone but apparently not. I want every inch of this town searched."

Johnny looked at him. "We shouldn't wait. We should start right now. We need to know if he's in town, or if he got hold of a horse and rode off. If he's still in town, we need to find him before he can hurt anyone else. If he has ridden away, then we need to get on his trail."

Tom nodded. "You're right. Let's get started now. I'd like to consider both you and Father still deputized."

Matt nodded his head. "Absolutely."

Danny appeared at the saloon doorway. "Me too. I want to help."

"Danny," Tom said. "You shouldn't be on your feet."

"Don't matter none. I want to help."

"All right. Let's knock on some doors and round up some men. We can send a rider into the valley, to the farms. Uncle Nathan, and Brewster and Ford."

Johnny walked up to him. "Except you can't be leading this posse. At least, not yet. Your brother might be dying and you need to be right here, waiting for word on him. You too," he looked at Matt. "And Danny."

Matt said, "He's right, son."

Tom shook his head. "The people of this town hired me to be their marshal. I can't abandon that job."

"You're not. You're human and your brother might be dying. No one would fault you for holding back and waiting to see if he's going to be all right."

"But who will lead the posse?"

Johnny said, "I will."

Johnny looked at Charles. "I want you to go knock on doors. There are miners who live here in town and can help with the search. And go to May's store and get Heck and May's husband Mack."

And Johnny looked at Harlan Carter. "I have a special job for you, if you don't mind."

Carter spoke in his tight-lipped way. "Anything you need."

28

QUINT SPENT the night making cold camp outside of town. He had stolen a horse and saddle from the livery stable the night before, and that horse had a bedroll tied to the saddle, so he was able to keep warm.

The livery stable attendant had been a boy who struck Quint as slow in the head. Quint wasn't normally one to feel pity or show mercy, but he didn't shoot the boy or stick a knife into him. Instead Quint left him tied up.

Quint knew it wouldn't be long before a posse would be coming after him, and he intended to ride out into the mountains and simply disappear for a while. But before he did, there was one last job he had to take care of. After all, he planned to eventually make his way back to California and get the rest of the money Aloysius Randall owed him. But to get paid, first he had to finish the job.

Actually, Randall had given him two jobs. One was to kill Judge Mack. The main reason was to get the judge out of the way. However, now that Judge Mather was in place, and Mather had been approved by Randall, and the old grizzly Judge Mack was leaving the area, Quint thought Randall might let him off the hook for not killing him. But the second job was one that had to be done if Quint hoped to be paid.

Randall had said to him, regarding his pay, "Half now, and half when the job is done."

And the part of the job still undone was burning the McCabe ranch house to the ground, unless Johnny McCabe agreed to sell to Randall. Because Hiram had double-crossed Randall at the trial, it was now impossible for Quint to approach Johnny without getting shot, so he figured maybe the boss would be satisfied with Quint burning the place down.

Besides, Quint liked fire.

The plan had been to kill some McCabes in the

process. However, the murder of McCabe's daughter had not gone as intended, and Quint heard talk that the man he shot had lived. Randall was going to have to settle for the deaths of any McCabes who might be caught in the house fire.

At the livery stable, the attendant had said that Johnny McCabe was in town, taking part in the posse that was searching for Quint. The one they called Charles was also in town, meaning only the women were at the house today. And Dusty, who was still recovering from Quint's bullet.

Quint figured he would get the drop on them, and leave them tied to chairs while he set the place on fire.

He saddled up and rode to the edge of the woods, where he could watch the house like he had done before.

He watched as the blonde-haired girl came out a door he figured was off of the kitchen and went to a chicken coop out back, and then a few minutes later she headed back to the kitchen. At least he figured it was her. At this distance it was hard to tell. The hair color had been right and looked like she was wearing a dress. Had to be a woman.

He figured the best way to do this was to just get on with it. Matches for the fire were in his vest pocket. The deputy's gun was tucked into the front of his belt, and five cartridges were loaded. He also had Hiram McCabe's little .22. Should be all he would need.

He clicked the horse forward to cover the quarter mile of open grassy terrain between the edge of the woods and the house.

No sign of any more activity at the house. The women were probably inside, preparing food or cleaning house or doing whatever it was women did. If what Quint had heard in town was accurate, Dusty wasn't even able to get out of bed, yet.

This should be easy, as long as no one saw him coming. After all, a woman could squeeze a trigger as well as a man could.

He reined up at the kitchen door. No sign of activity at all, other than smoke drifting from the chimney.

He swung out of the saddle and pulled the deputy's gun. His plan was to just walk into the house and aim the gun at the first woman he saw.

He climbed the back steps and tried the kitchen door. It wasn't locked.

He pushed it open and walked in, and he found Harlan Carter standing alone in the middle of the kitchen, facing the door. A gun was in his hand. And Quint knew who it was. He had known many men to have the cold eye of a killer, like this man did, but only he was this tall.

"Howdy," Carter said, and pulled the trigger.

The gun went off like a cannon, and the bullet slammed Quint in the chest. He stumbled a couple of steps backward and out the doorway, and down the steps.

Carter followed him. He kicked the revolver from Quint's hand and then pulled Hiram's gun from Quint's belt.

"You ain't too smart," Carter said.

Quint nodded. "Startin' to look that way."

And Quint breathed his last.

Johnny found Tom, Matt and Danny in the Second Chance, at a table. Each had a blue speckled cup of coffee in front of him.

Johnny said, "We searched the town as thoroughly we possibly can. We checked the livery stable and alleys. Every business there is, every house. Every barn. We found he had gotten the jump on Marvin at the livery stable and stole a horse. He didn't hurt Marvin but left him tied up."

Tom nodded. "He has a horse, then."

"Looks that way. I had Charles ride outside of town and cut for sign but he didn't find anything. If Quint left town, which it looks like he did, he probably rode away down Randall Road or Willbury Road, and the ground is too hard packed for tracks to be visible. I'm going to send two groups of men, one along each road, to see if we can find where he turned off."

Tom took a sip of coffee but, before he could say anything, Doc Martin came walking in. "Good, you're all here. Looks like your brother is going to be all right. I have to admit, Jack has surgical technique that is way beyond me. Hiram lost a lot of blood and it's going to be a long and slow recovery, and he won't be taking any train to California for a while, but I think he's out of the woods."

Matt said, "Maybe he can stay with Peddie and me at the cabin while he recuperates."

Tom looked at Johnny. "You should get some sleep. You didn't get any at all last night."

Johnny shook his head. "Not with Quint out there."

They heard the wet, muffled sort of *thump thump* that a horse's hooves make coming up behind the saloon from the woods. Someone was riding in along the small trail from the valley.

Johnny stepped out the saloon door, Tom immediately behind him, and they saw Harlan Carter riding around the corner to the front of the saloon. He was leading a horse with a body draped over the saddle and tied into place.

"Problem solved." Carter swung out of the saddle.

Tom said, "Is that Quint?"

Carter nodded his head. "Walked right into the kitchen through the back door, gun in hand. And he ran right into my bullet."

Johnny let out a long sigh, feeling like a weight had fallen from his shoulders. "You kept my family safe."

"Just like you asked me to do."

"I owe you."

Carter shook his head. "Just bein' neighborly."

29

THEY ALL GATHERED in a grassy spot out beyond the edge of town. Haley and Dusty were at the ranch, as Dusty wasn't quite ready for a ride to town yet, but most everyone else was there. Alisha Summers closed up the restaurant for the morning, and she had offered the place for the reception. She would stand beside Angie as the maid of honor. Jack would be standing by the Judge.

Johnny and Jessica were with Caleb and Elizabeth. Jonathan stood beside his grandfather. Bree was there, along with Charles.

Em had helped the Reverend Colter get things ready for the wedding, which pretty much involved finding a flat spot where they could fit a small crowd. Angie and the Judge both wanted an outdoor wedding.

With the crowd gathered, and everyone still waiting for the bride and groom, Colter said, "Miss Em, I was wondering if you would consent to allowing me to be your escort to the dance after this wedding. That is, if the bride and groom ever show up."

She smiled. "Why, Reverend, I would be delighted to."

"Well, there is one problem." He brought his fingers to his chin thoughtfully. We can't have you calling me *Reverend*, especially if I ask you to dance. Seems to me you should be calling me Jim."

"Jim it is."

Johnny said, "Here they come."

A buckboard made its way along the bumpy ground of the meadow. The Judge had the reins in his hands and Angie was beside him, hanging onto the edge of the wagon seat with both hands.

Judge Mack was in a jacket and bolo tie, and Angie wore a cream colored dress with a white lacy collar. It had been Em's, and Em wanted Angie to have it. Angie and the Judge had little money and everyone wanted to help. Aunt Ginny shortened up the dress a little because Em was two inches taller than Angie, and Cora and Elizabeth picked wild flowers for Angie's bouquet.

The Judge pulled the rig to a stop and Angie looked at the crowd with a beaming smile. "Thank you all for coming."

Aunt Ginny returned the smile. "We wouldn't miss it for the world, child."

Angie looked up at the sky. It was a deep, summertime blue with just a few wispy clouds at the western horizon. "And the sky is so perfect. I always wanted to get married outdoors and this is just how I dreamed the sky would be."

The Judge climbed to the ground and helped Angie down, and they walked over to where Colter waited for them. Jack stepped forward to stand by the Judge, and Alisha took her place beside Angie.

Colter looked to Tom. "If you would, Marshal?"

Tom stepped forward. He was in a jacket and a string tie, and in one hand was his Methodist Book of Worship.

"I can't think of a greater honor than taking part in this, as you both begin the next chapter of your lives."

Tom looked at Angie. "Are you sure you want to live the rest of your days with this old grizzly bear?"

She looked at Mack with a smile of pure joy. "I sure am."

"Then, let us begin." He opened his book. "Dearly beloved, we are gathered here in the sight of God..."

A man with a beard that fell to his belly sawed away on a fiddle and another plucked at a banjo with lightning fast fingers, and people danced and spun about. Some were attempting a Virginia Reel and others were just having a good time.

Matt stood with Johnny, a glass of scotch in his hand. "Too bad Joe isn't here. I think he'd like this shindig."

Johnny's brows rose. "Shindig? I don't think I've ever heard you use that word."

Matt grinned. "I'm trying to expand my vocabulary."

Then Matt saw Hiram at the balcony railing above. "He shouldn't be out of bed. Excuse me a minute."

Matt climbed the stairs. "Hiram, what are you doing out of bed?"

Hiram was in a nightshirt and robe, and he leaned with both hands on the balcony railing. "Well, a body can hardly sleep with half the town downstairs reeling and twirling about."

Matt nodded. "I was hoping you could get some rest here, until you were well enough to be taken out to my cabin for your convalescence. Maybe it wasn't such a good idea having the reception here."

Hiram shook his head. "It's fitting that they have it here. And I am grateful to Miss Alisha for allowing me to use one of the rooms. I can't pay her though, now that all of my funds have been transferred to accounts that don't have my name on them. Essentially, I am broke."

"Randall?"

Hiram nodded his head. "Most likely."

Matt said, "How does he have the authority to do that?"

"When you're as powerful as he is and willing to cross the line—whatever it takes to get the job done— you can do just about anything. He has judges in his pocket. Even here, Judge Mather was appointed because of some connection Randall apparently has with the Territorial Governor."

Matt shook his head. He leaned one hand on the railing and took a sip of whiskey. "I suppose you can't share a drink with me."

"Afraid not. That knife cut into my stomach wall. Jack is something of a medical wizard the way he sewed everything back together. Doc Martin said he had never seen anything like it. But I'll be on water, dry toast and thin, warm tea for a while."

Matt nodded.

Hiram said, "Also, I want to say that I appreciate the offer to convalesce at your home, but it's time we faced the facts. I am not your son. You know it and I know it."

"That's where you're wrong. One thing I've learned in my years living here in Montana, in this town, is that family isn't necessarily about blood. Take Johnny and his family. Em, down there," his gaze fell on Em who was dancing with the new minister, "she isn't actually related to him or Jessica at all, and yet they consider her to be their daughter. Cora is Jessica's because Jessica was a widow with a child when Johnny met her..."

Hiram nodded. "Bernard Swan's widow, from back in California. I remember."

"And yet, Johnny considers Cora his daughter."

Hiram looked at Matt. "What are you saying?"

"I'm saying that you're my son, if you want to be."

"It's not that simple. Not after the things I've done. The kind of man I am."

"Yes, it is that simple. You just stop being the man you were. Put it all behind you. Start over. And this is the place. The name of that saloon down the street, the Second Chance, it got that name for a reason."

Hiram ran a hand through his hair. "Redemption, hmm?"

Matt nodded his head. "Redemption."

"I don't know how I would even begin something like that."

"As with all journeys, you begin one step at a time."

Down below, Jonathan stood at the bar with a bottle of sarsaparilla in one hand. He was in jeans and boots, and a white shirt and bolo tie. The boy leaned with one elbow against the bar, looking as much like he could like a cowhand in for a bottle of beer on a Saturday night. Though he had to reach his elbow up a bit so it could touch the bar.

Johnny walked up. His intention was to get a refill of his glass of scotch, and then he noticed his grandson. "Jonathan, why aren't you dancing?"

The boy shrugged his shoulders. "Ain't no one here to dance with."

Johnny glanced across the room. Doc Martin's niece Peggy, who was about Jonathan's age, was standing with the doctor and his wife. Peggy was visiting from back East, and she wore a pink, checkered dress and had blonde hair that fell in ringlets to her shoulders.

She was looking at Jonathan, trying not to be obvious but was all too obvious to one who had danced this dance before, when he was younger.

Johnny said, "Peggy Martin seems to be watching you. Why don't you go over and ask her to dance?"

Jonathan gave the pained, defeated sigh that kids seemed to master so well. "Grampa, she's weird. She keeps looking at me and smiling."

"Jonathan, considering how tall you're getting, it won't be long before you start liking that kind of thing."

Jonathan took a sip of his sarsaparilla. "Grandpa?"

"Hmm?"

"I know my name ain't quite *John,* but I think I'd like it if folks started calling me Johnny."

Johnny couldn't help but smile. He hadn't been expecting that. "You should probably talk it over with your Ma and Pa, but if they're all right with it, then I would be honored."

A buckboard was packed with trunks and carpet bags. The Judge had tossed his saddle back there, and the horse he had ridden in on was tied to the back of the wagon.

Late afternoon had rolled upon them and the dance was still in progress without any sign of slowing down, but the Judge and Angie announced it was time for them to depart. The first night of their married life would be in a tent, in a camp they would set up somewhere along the trail, on their way to wherever they were going.

Alisha and Maybelle followed them out to the wagon, and Alisha took her in a hug. "You be well, Angie. And know that you're family and you both will always be welcome here."

Then it was Maybelle's turn. She pulled Angie in and wrapped her arms around her. "We've been through a lot together, the three of us. That creates a bond that will always be there."

Angie nodded her head. "You both were the only family I had for a long time."

Jack strolled out with Nina. "Take care, the both of you."

Angie gave him a hug. "Thank you so much for all you done for the Judge and me."

"It was entirely my pleasure."

Mack extended his hand and Jack shook it.

"Jack, you're a fine attorney. But you might make an even finer surgeon. Ever think of that?"

Jack shrugged his shoulders. "That's what Aunt Ginny has been telling me, but I made my decision years ago, when I rode away from medical school. The summer I met Nina." He looked over at her and she gave him a smile. "I think I'll keep on doing what I'm doing."

The Judge and Angie climbed into the wagon and the Judge snapped the reins and called out to the team, and the wagon began rolling forward.

Alisha wiped away a tear and Maybelle put an arm around her shoulders.

Jack said, "He and my Uncle Joe are two of a kind. There aren't many like them left."

He caught sight of Nathan Springer crossing the street toward them.

"McCabe, might I have a word with you?"

Nina touched Jack's arm. "I'll leave you two to talk."

She and Maybelle and Alisha headed back into the restaurant.

"What do you want, Springer?"

"I waited until the Judge and Miss Angie were gone. I didn't think they would want to see me."

Jack shrugged his shoulders. He didn't have a response to that.

"McCabe, it's difficult to say this, but it must be said. I think the Judge was right. About me, that is. I was looking negatively at you and your family. The charges I filed, well, part of the reason truly was pettiness on my part."

Jack knew how hard it was to say what Springer was trying to say, so instead of making him continue, Jack held his hand out.

Springer looked at him with a little surprise, then he shook Jack's hand.

Jack said, "Why not come inside and have a drink? Join the party."

"Would anyone really want me in there?"

Jack nodded his head. "You're part of this town too." He slapped Springer's shoulder. "Come on in."

Origen Scott had danced with Winifred Taylor, the daughter of the president of the bank. He had danced with her three times and he was still thinking about it as he stood at the bar later in the evening. The musicians had gone home and the dining room was now largely empty. Nina was helping Alisha and Maybelle clean up.

Jack said to him. "So, Orrie, I saw you dancing with Winnie earlier."

Orrie smiled and looked a little embarrassed. "I don't really know how to dance but she didn't seem to mind any."

"A good woman doesn't."

"Look, Jack, I know I was a little peeved at you earlier for stepping in and taking over the case. And I appreciate you enlisting my help later on. But I just wanted to say I'm glad you took over the case. You're five times the lawyer I'll ever be."

Jack shook his head. "Not necessarily. You need some seasoning, that's all."

Orrie shrugged. "I need *something*, that's for sure."

"Orrie, there's something I would like to ask you. Would you consider joining my firm? Maybe as a junior partner at first?"

Orrie blinked with surprise. "Really?"

Jack nodded. "It's a lot for one man to handle sometimes, and we did make a good team. The pay won't be much, until we build up some business, but I would like you on board."

"Well, gosh. I'm not making a whole lot of money on my own. My office rent eats up what little I make writing up contracts and wills and such. Miss Ginny has been letting me eat for free at the Second Chance."

"Then, what do you say?"

"What about that woman who works for you. Myrna Warren? She kind of scares me a little."

Jack grinned. "She kind of scares me too. But you'll get used to her."

Orrie held out his hand. "All right, then. You got yourself a deal."

And Jack shook the hand of his new junior partner.

30

JOSH AND TEMPERANCE HAD TAKEN the train with their infant son, to come to Jubilee for a visit. When Johnny and Jessica met them at the train station, Josh said, "Pa, I'd like to introduce you to your grandson, the newest McCabe."

Johnny took the child in his arms and looked into a pair of intense, blue eyes. "I can see you in him, Josh. Looks like he wants to wrestle down a calf and brand him, right here and now."

"Pa, meet John Thomas McCabe. Named after the greatest man I know."

Johnny looked at the boy and then at Josh. He didn't know quite what to say.

Jessica touched his arm. "If you could see yourself right now. I've never seen such a touching sight."

That evening, everyone was invited for supper. Josh had never met Hiram before.

"I've heard a lot about you," Josh said as they shook hands.

"Nothing good, I'm sure."

Josh shrugged and everyone laughed.

Temperance said, "Josh!"

He shook his head. "The family prides itself on honesty."

"That it does," Hiram said. "I haven't given the family much of a reason to speak well of me."

"Well," Josh grinned. "I've had my moments, too."

Dusty stood nearby. "I'll say."

And everyone laughed again.

It was early August, nearly a month since Hiram had been wounded, and Haley and Jack were both satisfied that he was recovering at a good pace. Dusty had moved back to his and Haley's house and was also recovering quickly.

After dinner, with a fire crackling in the great

stone hearth, everyone moved into the parlor. Ginny sat in a rocker by the fire, with a glass of white wine in one hand. Jessica drank little wine, but tonight she joined Ginny and sat on the nearby sofa.

Jack held little John Thomas in his arms and said, "So, what's he going to be called? Johnny, like his grandpa?"

Johnny glanced over at Jonathan, who stood nearby. A little man, in his jeans and riding boots. Johnny said, "No, that name's already taken, twice over."

Johnny nodded to him and Jonathan smiled.

Hiram hadn't yet been cleared by Haley or Jack to drink whiskey, and he wasn't sure he ever wanted to go back to it. He figured he had consumed too much of it over the years, maybe in an attempt to hide himself from the path he had been following. But they did clear him for a glass of white wine. So, with a glass in hand, he left the crowd behind and wandered out to the porch.

The air was clear and the stars seemed so close he thought he could almost reach out and touch one.

Matt stepped up behind him. "I saw you come out here. You all right?"

Hiram nodded. "I just feel a little out of place in this crowd."

"I hope one day you won't. You *are* family, after all."

"And yet, for many years I was perceived as the enemy. I am starting to see that maybe I was my own worst enemy. Oh, I had money. Mother made certain of that. And I had power. But I was not truly living. These people in the house tonight—altogether they couldn't put forth the assets I had out in California. And yet, they have something I never had."

"And what is that?"

"Happiness."

Matt stood beside his son and they looked off at the Montana sky.

Hiram said, "I'm starting to see why you and

Uncle Johnny like it so much out here."

Matt nodded his head. "There's nothing like a Montana sky on a clear, summer night."

He held a glass of scotch in one hand and he took a sip. "You know, you can have happiness, too."

"How?"

"Right here, with all of us. Live your life here. Contribute to the community and become one of us."

"But would they have me?"

"I don't see how they could say no, if you're sincere in your intentions. Like I said earlier, this seems to be a place of second chances. I found my second chance on life here, with Peddie. Johnny has his with Jessica. And you know Carter Harding?"

Hiram nodded. "I've met him. A scary individual."

"I probably shouldn't say this, because if it ever got out he would be facing a noose. But his real name is Harlan Carter. He was a raider and outlaw in the Kansas-Missouri area, years ago. He's wanted for murder many times over. And there's Vic Falcone, who runs a farm off toward the center of the valley."

Hiram nodded his head. "That's the same name as an outlaw who was also wanted by the law."

"He *is* that outlaw. Or he was at one time. Now he and his wife attend pot luck dinners at church. Sam Middleton has a past. Your own cousin Dusty was raised by outlaws. And then there's me. I turned a blind eye to the activities of my late wife, and she hurt a lot of people, most of all you. But here, we all seem to find a second chance."

"What is it about this place?"

Matt shrugged his shoulders. "Oh, I don't think it's the place itself. I think it's more of a concept. After all, good will is contagious. And forgiveness is a thing of the Bible. God forgives us, if we approach him repentantly, sincerely regretting our human failings and the things we do wrong because of them. As it says in the Psalms, he shows us his mercy and grants us his salvation."

Hiram blinked with surprise. "The Bible? You?"

Matt nodded. "I'm not the man I was, back in California, hiding in my study and smoking expensive cigars and running a cattle empire, while my late former wife spread corruption everywhere she could, especially within my eldest son. It's about seeking God's forgiveness, but part of that is about forgiving yourself."

"Do you forgive yourself?"

Matt shrugged again. "For most of it. I have a hard time forgiving myself when I think of what I let Verna do to you. What I let her teach you. I should have taken a firmer hand. You suffered for it, and I am so sorry."

Hiram took a sip of wine. "Maybe you should take your own advice, Father, and learn to forgive yourself. I may not have inside me much of what makes a man a McCabe, but I can tell you this—I don't think I'm the same man I was when I first arrived here, a month and a half ago."

They stood in silence for a few moments.

Matt said, "So, what are your plans?"

"I really don't know."

"I know one thing. I hope you stay here. I've been talking with Peddie, and she said she feels the same way. I'm sure everyone inside the house would agree."

Hiram chuckled and shook his head. "I hardly think so, Father. I may have learned a thing or two about real integrity these past couple of months, but can a leopard truly change its spots?"

"Did you ever think that the way you were was just based on what you learned from your mother? That maybe you're actually a good man at heart?"

"Frankly, no. I was a powerful man, and a decisive one, but I never considered myself a good man."

"Maybe it's time you start being one."

"And how do I do that?"

Matt leaned one hand on the porch rail. "By dismissing your past and looking at today, and tomorrow. Say to yourself, *Today I am going to be a good man.* And do the right things."

"You make it sound so easy."

Matt shook his head. "Nothing easy about it at all. I don't know if I could have found a new life if not for Peddie."

"Well, I don't have a good woman like that in my life."

"Maybe you don't need one. I think maybe you're stronger than I am."

"What would ever make you think that?"

"Gut feeling. My father taught me that you have to trust your gut, because your mind can be fooled by fast-talking and self-doubt, but your gut is your gut. It won't lie to you. Learn to trust it, son."

Those words fell onto Hiram and worked their way into him. And suddenly his future seemed plain and clear.

"Haley and Jack have told me that I'm nearly well enough for travel. Aloysius Randall has taken all of my assets, but I withdrew some cash before he did so and have enough for a round ticket to California. I have some business to take care of there."

Matt looked at him. "A round ticket?"

Hiram nodded. "I think maybe I'll come back here. Maybe settle into this community. Maybe learn firsthand what second chances are all about."

31

HIRAM WORE his jacket and tie, and a bowler was on his head. He sat in the saddle and his father rode beside him, as their horses worked their way down the mountain trail toward Jubilee.

"Son, are you sure you have enough money for the journey?"

Hiram nodded. "Thanks, but I'll be fine. I also have my pocket revolver. Tom returned it to me after Mister Carter shot Quint."

Matt smiled. "Always travel with a gun."

Hiram returned the smile. "It seems I did learn a thing or two from you after all."

"I'm proud of you, you know."

"Because I'm turning away from the life I once led?"

Matt shook his head. "Because you're looking deep within yourself and trying to become a better man."

They rode in silence for a few moments, then Matt said, "You know another reason I like about having you around?"

Hiram shook his head.

"I can use what your Uncle Joe calls ten-dollar words and you don't chastise me for it."

Hiram laughed. "I suppose that's another thing we share."

At the train station, Matt shook Hiram's hand. "Be safe, son."

"I will, Father. I hope to see you in a couple of weeks."

Hiram traveled with only the carpet bag that he had carried when he first arrived in town. It was in his seat beside him as he sat on the train and looked out the window, and watched the town of Jubilee slide away. A town he thought was dreadful when he first arrived but, now—he had to admit—it had claimed a piece of his heart.

He had talked little with Father about the business he had to wrap up in California. But he knew what he had to do, and he felt only he could do it.

Aloysius Randall was a tall man with a narrow frame and a hairline that was thinning.

He sat at his desk, reviewing ledgers for the portion of his empire that was devoted to cattle. What was once the McCarty Ranch and had become the Circle M when Matt McCabe ran it, but now belonged to Randall. He was putting together information so he could make an offer on the largest cattle outfit in California, a ranch outside of Stockton that was even bigger than the Circle M.

His desk was not of the old school roll top variety but the newer flat top that was coming into style. After all, he liked to see himself as a man of the future.

There was a knock at his office door and he looked up from the open ledger book. "What is it?"

The door opened and a young man stepped in. He wore spectacles and his hair was greased down and parted in the middle.

Randall snapped at him. "Hodges, I told you I don't want to be disturbed. I *never* like to be disturbed."

Hodges looked nervous. Afraid. Randall was pleased. Employees who were afraid of him gave him the proper amount of respect.

Hodges said, "I'm sorry, sir, but there is a Hiram McCabe here to see you."

Randall blinked with surprise and he rose to his feet. "Hiram McCabe?"

Hiram pushed past Hodges and stepped into the room. "Thought I was dead, didn't you?"

Randall raised his brows in a sort of shrug. "Well, I had hoped."

Hodges stood in the doorway looking like he wanted to be anywhere other than here.

Randall said to him, "That's all, Hodges."

A very grateful Hodges stepped out and closed the door.

Randall said, "Yes, I thought you were dead."

"The man you sent to do the job, Gabe Quint, is dead."

"No matter. Now I won't have to pay him the rest of what I owed him."

"I must admit, I was a little surprised to find you here at the office. I would have thought you would be preparing your defense in court."

Randall smiled. "Defense for what?"

Hiram nodded his head as it dawned on him. "Judge Mather never contacted the state Attorney General, did he? Quint had said the judge was in your pocket."

"Buying a few judges is money well spent."

"Randall, I want you to leave my family alone. I want you to leave the entire town of Jubilee alone."

Randall smiled. "Oh you do, do you? Are you telling me you have finally grown a spine?"

Randall stepped out from behind his desk. "Listen to me, McCabe. You're irrelevant to me. You were only relevant until I had full possession of your assets. You thought you were one of the most powerful men in California, but you were never on a level with me. And you know why? Because you don't have what it takes to make the hard decisions. You value life too much, where I value only one life—mine. And that's how you need to be if you want to rise to the levels that I am rising to. Your assets are mine, and you can't have them back. Simple as that. You can take me to court if you like but you can't win because, quite simply, I own the judges, and the governor is an ally of mine."

Randall pulled a pocket watch from his vest. "I will own the McCabe Ranch, and the McCabe family will be dead, especially that self-styled gunfighter and the daughter they call Bree. Gabe Quint couldn't do the job, so I'll find someone who can. In the end, I win. I always win. Get used to it."

He flipped open the watch and glanced at the time. "Now I have to be leaving. I have an appointment. You see, Hiram, I have a girl waiting. She's young, not quite fifteen. But then, I like them young."

He grabbed a bowler from a hat stand in one corner. "Remember, I always get my way. I always win."

"No man is above the law."

Randall stopped at the door. He had been about to reach for the doorknob but now he turned to face Hiram. "Are you serious? Listen to yourself. It's not about the law, Hiram. It's about money and power, and I have both. I'm not above the law. I *am* the law."

He turned away again and reached for the doorknob.

Hiram said, "It's clear you have to be stopped."

"Oh? And how are you going to do that?"

"Any way I have to."

Randall glanced back over his shoulder and saw a small revolver in Hiram's hand.

"And what do you think you're going to do with that?"

"Rid the world of a problem that it should have been rid of long ago."

Randall turned to face him. "You don't have what it takes to pull that trigger. And do you know why? Because you're weak. Your mother knew it and I know it. You don't have the strength to make the hard decisions. That strength is what powerful men have, and you don't have it. Your mother knew it all too well."

Hiram cocked the pistol. "You knew nothing of my mother."

"Are you serious? She was the most powerful woman in California. I was rising quickly on the ladder of power. We sat and cut many deals together. The takeover of the Virginia Middleton fortune and paying judges so I have them in my pocket were actually her ideas. McCabe's daughter refused me, once. Embarrassed me. You don't do that. It must be known that if you refuse me or embarrass me, it's a death sentence. In fact," he grinned, "your mother orchestrated my entire takeover of your assets."

"No."

"I waited a few years before I did it, to make sure it was necessary. But it became clear to me that it was."

Randall placed his hat on his head. "It's been my pleasure to give you a little history lesson. Now I'm going to spend some time with the little girl who's waiting for me. And when I'm done, I'll go to work on the takeover of the McCabe Ranch and the death of Johnny McCabe and his daughter. Not because they stand in my way, but just as an example to others."

Randall's gaze dropped to the gun that was still in Hiram's hand. "And put that thing away before you hurt yourself, will you?"

Hiram pulled the trigger and Randall felt the bullet hit him in the chest. Hiram fired again, knowing a single bullet might not do the trick because of the small caliber of the gun. Randall took a step back as the second bullet struck only two inches from the first.

Hiram said, "You're not quite as powerful as you think you are. There is always a way to stop a man."

Hiram fired again.

Randall's eyes were wide, and his voice was thin and raspy. "You'll never get away with this. You'll go to prison."

"That may be, but you have to be stopped."

Randall staggered back one more step and bumped into the door that was still closed. Then his knees went weak and he crashed to the floor.

He tried to call out, but his voice wasn't much more than a whisper. "Hodges!"

And then the life went from his eyes and he stopped breathing.

Hodges opened the door and tentatively peeked in. "I heard gunshots."

His gaze fell on Randall's body and then the gun in Hiram's hand. "Is he dead?"

Hiram nodded.

Hodges stepped fully in. "It's after five. The building is mostly empty. It's quite possible no one else heard the shots."

He stepped aside, clearing the doorway. "I saw nothing. Get clear of this building and go. I'll wait an hour before I call the constables. As far as I know, I'm the only one who knows you were here. I'll tell the constables I stepped outside and smoked a cigar, and that must have been when some unknown intruder shot him."

"Why?"

Hodges shrugged his shoulders. "Seems to me it's for the greater good."

Hiram slid the revolver back into its holster inside his jacket. "I am indebted to you."

Hodges shook his head. "It is I, and many others, who are indebted to you. Now go."

Hiram glanced down at the body once more, and then he stepped past Hodges and was gone.

32

MONTANA COULD BE warm in the late summer, but this was a rainy afternoon and it had turned quite cool. Tom had a fire going in the stove at his office and coffee brewing in the kettle.

Danny sat behind his desk, going through a stack of reward fliers that had arrived by train. New ones to add to the old ones that had been here for two months.

"Hey, look at this." He held one flier out for them all to see. "Gabriel Quint, wanted in Texas for murder. Five hundred dollar reward. Wonder if Mister Carter can claim the reward."

Tom shook his head. "Not without risking a federal marshal being sent here for him."

Danny nodded his head. "Well we don't need this one on the wall."

He crumpled it into a ball and tossed it into a small barrel by his desk.

Matt sat at the edge of the desk with a cigar in his hand. Not the expensive type of cigar he once smoked in a previous life, but it was good enough. He certainly wouldn't want that life back just to get a good cigar.

Danny said, "I hear Miss Alisha's hired a new girl to wait tables."

Tom nodded his head. "I suppose she had to, with Miss Angie gone."

Matt took a draw of the cigar. "Have you given any thought to your future, Tom? Looks like statehood is going to pass, and then we'll be needing a county sheriff."

"We might be getting ahead of ourselves on that."

Matt shook his head. "No, I don't think so. I think it's going to pass before the year's out."

Danny said, "I wonder what that'll do for life around here?"

"We'll have all the benefits of statehood. We'll be able to vote in presidential elections. We have sent delegates to Congress but they had no vote, but once we have statehood we'll be electing actual, fully functioning senators and congressmen. And the state will be divided into counties. The talk is this might be called McCabe County." He looked at Tom. "You could be running for sheriff of the county that bears your family's name."

The door opened again, and Hiram stepped in.

Matt looked up with surprise. "Hiram."

Hiram stood in the doorway looking at each of them. "You weren't sure you'd ever see me again, were you?"

"Well..." Tom wasn't sure what to say.

Matt said, "We were hoping."

Hiram stepped in and they all shook hands with him.

Matt said, "I figured one of the reasons you were going back was to see Aloysius Randall. How did it go with him?"

"Apparently the news hasn't reached here yet. Three days ago, Randall was murdered in his office. Shot down."

"You don't say."

Hiram nodded. "You live like he did, do the things he did, you're bound to make enemies."

He reached into his jacket and pulled out his small Smith & Wesson. "By pure coincidence, of course, he was shot by the same caliber bullet that this holds. Three of them, in fact. And I am now three bullets short."

Matt looked at his son. "Hiram..."

"I did what had to be done, Father. It wasn't about revenge or him taking possession of my assets. It was about stopping a monster, and I knew of no other way to do it. It seems to me that sometimes you just have to do a job, as unpleasant as that job might be."

He slid the gun back into his jacket, and he looked at his father. "When I was recuperating, you and I sat many a night on the front porch of your cabin, and you told me about the family. What was it Miss Ginny called the McCabe men? Knights in buckskin? And you said Uncle Johnny just calls them gunhawks."

Matt nodded.

"I know it's not right to shoot down a man like that, when he's not drawing his gun against you. But in a way, Randall was drawing on all of us. He was planning to send more men like Quint here to murder Uncle Johnny and Bree. He had Judge Mather in his pocket. It was the only way I knew to stop him."

Tom said, "Sounds like you did what you had to do."

"Maybe it turns out I have a little gunhawk blood in me after all."

Matt nodded his head to Hiram, and Hiram nodded back.

Danny said, "What's next for you, Hiram?"

Hiram shrugged his shoulders. "I don't know. After my trip to California, all the money I have left to my name is pocket change. One dollar and thirty-six cents."

The coffee was ready, so Tom walked over to the stove and moved the pot from the center to the edge. "Well, the Town Council has finally coughed up the money for me to hire a second deputy. I think the prospect of statehood is making them feel a little more confident and they're loosening up the purse strings."

"Are you offering me a job?"

Tom took two cups, handed one to Hiram and poured coffee in them both. "It's a tedious job and often thankless."

Danny rolled his eyes. "Is it ever."

"The pay isn't good. Hardly enough to pay the rent."

Matt said, "You can stay with Peddie and me as long as you need to."

"But it's good, honest work. You'll be working not for yourself, but to keep the town safe."

Hiram took a sip of coffee. "I don't know anything about being a deputy." He looked at Tom. "But I think

I'd like to learn."

"Well, then the job is yours."

Hiram then took a chair, and he did something he had never done before. He sat and chatted over coffee with his father and his brothers.

Made in the USA
Monee, IL
04 November 2025